LIZZIE
and THE
LOST BABY

Lizzie
and THE
Lost Baby

Cheryl Blackford

Houghton Mifflin Harcourt
Boston New York

Library of Congress Cataloging-in-Publication Data
Blackford, Cheryl.
Lizzie and the lost baby / by Cheryl Blackford.
p. cm.
Summary: Evacuated to a remote Yorkshire valley during World War
II, a homesick ten-year-old English girl discovers an abandoned baby
and befriends a gypsy boy, despite local prejudice.
ISBN 978-0-544-57099-3
1. World War, 1939–1945—Evacuation of civilians—Juvenile fiction. 2.
World War, 1939–1945—England—Yorkshire—Juvenile fiction.
[1. World War, 1939–1945—Evacuation of civilians—Fiction. 2. World
War, 1939–1945—England—Yorkshire—Fiction. 3. Friendship—Fiction.
4. Romanies—Fiction. 5. Abandoned children—Fiction. 6. Prejudices—
Fiction. 7. Yorkshire (England)—History—20th century—Fiction. 8.
Great Britain—History—George VI, 1936–1952—Fiction.] I. Title.
PZ7.B53232Li 2016
[Fic]—dc23
2014047003

Manufactured in the United States of America
DOC 10 9 8 7 6 5 4 3 2 1
4500572735

For Mum and Dad.
And for David, who has
always believed in me.

Chapter One

LIZZIE

EVERY WINDOW on the train had been painted black, blocking any possible view of the passing scenery. Lizzie knew the paint was necessary to hide the train's lights from German planes, but she wished she could see outside where there might be farmland, mountains, or rivers to watch. Instead, as the train sped along the tracks, all Lizzie saw was her own frizzy-haired reflection in the blank black rectangle of glass.

Children from Lizzie's school were crammed into the train carriage. Some sat on suitcases in the aisle while others bickered and jostled for room on the crowded seats. Some sat blank-faced with their gas masks slung over their shoulders and their possessions in their laps. A few of the older children played a card game using a suitcase for a table. A tiny girl cried, "Mummy, I want my mummy," over and over again. Lizzie couldn't reach the girl to comfort her — there were too many other children in the way.

In the strange cocoon of the carriage, Lizzie had lost all sense of time. It had been early morning when she'd taken Peter's hand, said goodbye to their mother, and climbed onto the double-decker bus outside their school in Hull. It had still been morning when the bus had stopped at the railway station and she'd guided Peter to a seat on the packed train. They'd long ago eaten their potted meat sandwiches, but Lizzie's watch had stopped at eleven o'clock, and she had no idea how many hours had passed since then on the rattling, clattering train.

"Look after Peter, love," her mother had said after giving Lizzie a final kiss. "Don't let them send you to different homes. Seven's too young for him to be on his own."

Lizzie had turned in a sudden panic on the bus step and said, "Do we have to go?"

Her mother's eyes had glistened. "Yes, love, you

do. We're at war now. It won't be safe in Hull — the Germans will bomb the city."

"Why can't you come with us?"

"I have to stay behind, Lizzie. Parents aren't allowed to go." Her mother had painted a false smile on her face and said, "You'll have such an adventure in the country. You'll be safe there, and I'm sure someone kind will take you in."

Lizzie had heard this so many times from her parents and her teacher, Mrs. Scruton, that she could recite the speech herself. She knew that city children had to be evacuated to keep them safe from the bombs. She knew that most of their fathers would join the army to fight the Germans. She knew that most of their mothers would take the place of the men in the factories and offices. But knowing the reasons why she had to leave didn't help — Lizzie would rather face the bombs than live in a strange place with people she didn't know. After all, they had a bomb shelter now.

Before he'd left to join the army, her father had removed the roses from their back garden and dug a big hole in the lawn. He'd made walls using half-buried sheets of corrugated metal and a roof from more of the metal sheets before mounding a huge pile of soil over the top. When the bomb shelter was finished, he'd put two camp beds inside for her mother and grandmother to sleep on and a little Primus stove for them to make tea.

"That'll do nicely," he'd said. "You'll be safe in there."

The shelter was cramped and damp and probably full of spiders. Still, if it would keep Mummy and Nana safe in a bombing raid, wouldn't it keep Lizzie and Peter safe too?

But Lizzie hadn't been given a choice to stay.

She shifted on her seat and pushed Peter's lolling head into a more comfortable position on her shoulder. He made little whimpering noises in her ear as he slept and his head was heavy, but she was grateful for the relief from his endless questions.

"Where are we going?" he'd asked as the train pulled out of Hull Station. "Why didn't Mummy come with us? Who will look after us?"

Lizzie's stomach flipped a somersault. Who *would* look after them?

She reached into her school satchel and felt for Nana's gift. Her fingers gripped the smooth hard box for comfort. Inside the box, nestled on a bed of white satin, was a beautiful new fountain pen.

"That's not fair," Peter had complained when Nana gave it to her. "Her birthday's not for ages."

But Nana had patted his head and said, "Hush, now. We don't know if you'll be home in time for Lizzie's birthday, so she'd better have it now. Besides, she'll need it to write me lots of lovely letters."

Nana had given Lizzie a whole sheet of stamps — so many stamps. Would they really be gone long enough for Lizzie to write that many letters?

She rested her feet on their suitcase, leaned her head against the back of the leather seat, and closed her eyes, but she couldn't stop the thoughts. What if the people in the country weren't kind? What if they didn't like her? What if she couldn't look after Peter?

What if you stop worrying? Nana would say.

How would Lizzie manage without Nana to reassure her?

We're two peas in a pod, you and me. Nana said that all the time, which was funny, because Nana was short and stout like a barrel on legs, and Lizzie was as thin as a rake.

Who would make Lizzie laugh now? She twisted a loop of hair back and forth between her fingers as the train swayed and rattled on its relentless way.

She woke to a sudden jerk and the harsh squeal of brakes.

Mrs. Scruton stepped into their carriage. She took the hand of the little girl who'd been crying for her mother and said, "This is our stop, children."

Lizzie picked up their suitcase and poked Peter when he almost left his gas mask on the seat. Together they clambered down onto the platform. A long line of train carriages stretched through the small station, and Lizzie wondered if there were any children left in Hull.

Billows of steam wafted from the hissing engine. A man wearing a dark uniform and cap waved a green flag and blew his whistle. The train, their last connection with home, pulled out of the station and disappeared into the misty distance.

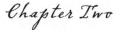

Chapter Two

ELIJAH

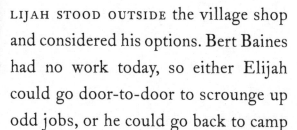

ELIJAH STOOD OUTSIDE the village shop and considered his options. Bert Baines had no work today, so either Elijah could go door-to-door to scrounge up odd jobs, or he could go back to camp and explain to his mother why he had no money for their supper. A steady drizzle fell from dense gray clouds; there wasn't much chance he'd find work in this weather.

He looked down at Jack, a bedraggled bundle by his feet. "What do you think, boy? Shall us go home?"

The little tan-and-white terrier wagged his tail.

The shop bell jangled, and Colonel Clegg

stepped out. He thrust his chest forward. "You there! What are you doing? Can't you read what that says?" The colonel stabbed his finger at a sign hanging on the door.

Block letters danced across Elijah's vision. He read "No," but the other word defeated him. He planted his hands on his hips and stared at the colonel.

"I suppose you're illiterate like the rest of your lot. The sign says 'No Loitering.' If you're not here to purchase something, clear off."

"I'm not doing nowt wrong."

The words escaped on a wave of resentment. Elijah instantly regretted them; the colonel could make plenty of trouble for him.

There's times when you must swallow yer pride fer the good of all, my Elijah. That's what Granddad Ambrose would say.

Elijah looked down at the ground. "I were just looking fer work, sir. Didn't mean no harm."

"Work. Humph! That's rare for you Gypsies. You're lazy, the lot of you."

Then Colonel Clegg tilted his head to one side. He looked like a fat pigeon waiting for crumbs. "Go and wait at the station. When you hear the train, come and get me. I'll be at the Coach and Horses."

He flicked a threepenny bit onto the ground. "There'll be another when you fetch me."

Now that Dad had gone off to join the army, money was tight. Sixpence was better than nothing. Elijah picked up the coin and wiped it across his trouser legs to remove all traces of the colonel. Then he went to wait for the train.

The wind moaned and swirled through the nooks and crannies of the deserted platform. Water dripped from the eaves of the station roof and puddled on the ground. Elijah tried to forget the colonel's ugly remarks. He was used to the prejudice that most of the Gorgios, the settled folk, displayed toward the traveling people.

Ignore them. Words can't hurt you, Granddad Ambrose would say.

But Elijah thought of the times when their men had been arrested for no reason and their wagons made to move on by the police. Granddad Ambrose was wrong — hateful words led to angry actions.

Elijah straightened his cap, turned up his collar, and squinted down the line. He saw a faint thickening of the mist in the distance. When he was sure the cloud was steam and not a trick of the light, he raced to the pub.

The colonel flicked a second coin at Elijah before strutting off down the street. Elijah followed him and watched from behind the station gate, curious to see why the colonel was so interested in this train.

Whatever Elijah expected to see, it certainly wasn't the crowd of children who poured onto the platform. Some of them were clean and dressed like townies; others were grubby and scruffy. The smaller ones carried dolls and teddy bears; the bigger ones carried satchels and suitcases. Every child carried a gas mask.

The colonel and a woman who seemed to be in charge marched the children toward the village. Who they were and why they'd come were a mystery.

Elijah hurried past the churchyard and trudged down the lane to camp. The horses, their spotted coats slick with rain, lifted their heads and whinnied as he passed.

He vaulted the gate into the field, catching a shower of glistening droplets from the overhanging hawthorn bush, and sprinted through the muck. Two of Mammy's bantam hens, foraging by the fire pit, squawked and flapped out of his way.

Streams of rainwater ran down the curved tops of the eight bow-top wagons lined up near the river — one wagon for each family in their group. The bow tops were all muted greens and grays, like the sodden trees, but Mammy's Reading wagon was different — its yellow steps and cheery red door promised warmth and comfort.

Elijah waved at Tyso and Israel, sheltering in one of the tents beside the wagons, and climbed Mammy's steps. He tucked his wet boots behind the water-filled milk churn on the little porch and stepped through the doorway. Angela and May stood beside the stove warming their hands while Mammy sipped a mug of tea. Her hawking basket sat on the little table by the window, still filled with the carved wooden flowers and clothes pegs she sold.

"Did you sell much?" he asked.

She shook her head. "I didn't tell any fortunes either. The weather's made folks bad-tempered. What did you bring me?"

"Only sixpence," he said, adding the coins to the pitiful collection in an old jam jar.

"Fried taters and onions fer dinner again, then," Mammy said.

"I tried me best, but Bert Baines had no work, and no one else will hire the likes of us."

She touched Elijah's arm. "You never gives up — just like yer dad."

The compliment warmed him better than a bowl of stew, but so far he hadn't been able to make more than a fraction of the money Dad used to make.

Mammy took a brush to Angela's long hair, working out the tangles despite her squeaks of protest. "Yer granddad said there's been children sent here."

"I seen them get off the train. There were nigh on a hundred of them. Where are their mams and dads?"

Mammy tied a pink ribbon in Angela's hair. "Government said they had to stay behind in the cities. It's right sad to think on sending yer little uns away like that. Even if it is to keep them safe from bombs."

Elijah heard a happy gurgle from the far end of the wagon. He pulled the heavy red curtain to one side. Rose giggled at him and kicked her chubby legs in the air. He picked her up from the bed and smoothed her hair — hair the color of crows' feathers, just like his own. She had dark eyes, dimples at the corners of her mouth, and tiny ears that stuck out at the top.

You two are the spitting image of each other, Dad used to say.

Elijah cuddled her and gave her a kiss. "That one's from Dad."

A familiar figure blocked the doorway.

"I've brought these fer you, Vi. To fill the little uns' bellies." Bill dangled a floppy pair of rabbits from his meaty fist. "They'll make a grand stew." He grinned, displaying the gap where he'd lost a tooth in a fight.

Elijah looked away. All the seasonings in the world would not make that rabbit taste good to him.

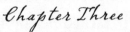

Chapter Three

LIZZIE

THE GRAY SKY LEAKED a steady drizzle over the fields on the far side of the railway tracks. The station name had been painted over to confuse any invading Germans, so Lizzie had no idea where the train had stopped, but the station building was small and there was only one platform. She stood on tiptoe to look over the white wooden fence and saw stone houses, different from the rows of brick houses that lined the streets of Hull.

A short man wearing a tweed suit and round, thick-framed spectacles approached Mrs. Scruton and pointed at a school with rows of blacked-out windows beneath its slate roof. The silent children followed Mrs. Scruton and the man through the schoolyard and into the gymnasium, where a crowd of chattering adults had gathered.

"Attention!" the short man shouted.

The chattering stopped.

He turned to the children. "I am Colonel Clegg. This is Swainedale. You will be billeted here in North Yorkshire until we win the war. Stand still until you are selected." He barked out the final sentence.

The adults in the gymnasium began to inspect the children. Neat girls and muscular boys were quickly selected. A broad-shouldered man with a sour expression scrutinized Lizzie, but turned away when he saw Peter.

Lizzie spotted Samuel Rosen, looking lost and miserable as usual, waiting at the edge of the crowd. He wore short trousers that were too tight and a jacket that was too big. His eyes were huge in his pale face as he cast nervous glances from one adult to the next. Lizzie watched as a couple approached him. The man had sun-browned skin, a mustache flecked with gray, and mud on the cuffs of his trousers. The pink-cheeked woman draped a raincoat over Samuel's shoulders and gave him a comforting smile. Kindness radiated from them as they led him out of the room.

Lizzie chewed her lip. Why had the couple chosen Samuel instead of her and Peter? Was she too thin? Were they too untidy? Was Peter's nose too runny? She straightened her hat, pulled up her brother's wrinkled knee socks, and gave him a handkerchief.

A tall man in a police uniform strode toward her.

Lizzie swallowed. Had she done something wrong?

But a plump woman wearing a shabby raincoat and a scarf decorated with prancing horses took the policeman's elbow and whispered in his ear. She led him away from Lizzie and Peter and toward a tiny girl in a neat navy-blue coat.

Lizzie stared at the joins between the planks in the wooden floor. What if no one wanted them?

A large pair of shiny black shoes appeared in her field of view. "Hello there. I'm Fred Arbuthnot and this is my wife, Madge," a gruff voice said.

Lizzie looked up to find the policeman leaning forward and reading the nametags pinned to their coats. "Lizzie and Peter Dewhurst. How old are you two?"

"I'm ten and Peter's seven."

"Well, you're to come with us," the policeman said. "Our Madge here will take you home. I've to stay and keep this lot under control." He turned and strode around the room, greeting the adults and patting children on the head.

The woman in the raincoat stretched her lips into a thin smile. "You'd better not expect anything fancy from us. Plain food and plain talk, that's what you'll get. Come along." She picked up their suitcase, turned on her heels, and walked toward the door.

Lizzie and Peter followed.

Outside, the drizzle had turned to a steady soaking rain. Madge heaved their suitcase into a wicker basket fastened to the front of a battered bicycle. She looked up at the sky and tied her scarf over her hair. "You'd better hurry. It's a mile up the dale to our house, and this is set in for the day."

"What's a dale?" Peter asked.

"Yorkshire born and you don't know what a dale is!" Madge shook her head as if her worst fears about them had been confirmed. "Dale's another name for a valley. This here's Swainedale. Up there's

Blackfriar's Moor. And our house is up there." She waved her arm at the misty distance.

Lizzie squinted through the rain. She'd never seen moorland, but from the descriptions in her favorite book, *The Secret Garden*, she thought it must be rough and wild. She'd have to wait for the weather to clear before she could see for herself.

They walked on past honey-colored stone cottages with neat vegetable gardens.

Madge turned up her collar. "This weather's not fit for ducks."

Rain dripping from the brim of his cap, Peter grinned up at her. "Or frogs or geese or tadpoles."

Madge smiled down at him.

Peter had charmed Madge without even trying. It was easy for him with his long eyelashes and cheeky smile — he didn't have rabbit teeth and hair that frizzed in the damp.

Madge pushed her squeaky bike past the houses on the outskirts of the village and up a muddy lane lined on either side by thick hedges. Lizzie and Peter trudged on, following Madge past desolate fields surrounded by walls made of mossy rocks piled higgledy-piggledy upon one another. Lizzie's satchel strap dug into her shoulder, and her socks were soon soaking wet, but she didn't dare complain.

They walked for a long time without seeing any more buildings until a bleak row of gray stone houses materialized out of the mist in front of them. The houses looked out of place, as if a giant had picked them up and dropped them in the middle of the dripping valley instead of in some town or city.

Madge trundled her bike along a rutted muddy lane at the back of the houses and leaned it against a wall next to a blue door. "This is our house, but you're not staying with us because Susan, my daughter, is home again. You'll not see much of her though. She works for the colonel, and he keeps her busy until all hours."

She hesitated before saying, "You're to stay next door with our Elsie. She's not been well. Mind you don't upset her."

Madge opened a green door at the back of the next house, and Lizzie stepped through it into a chilly kitchen. She removed her shoes, leaving them on the bristly doormat, and stood in her wet socks on a cold flagstone floor.

A woman with straggly hair sat in a rocking

chair beside the stove. She wore a baggy cardigan over a flower-print dress. Younger and thinner than Madge, she looked frail, as if she would crumple at a touch.

Madge raised her voice and spoke slowly. "Elsie, this here's Lizzie and Peter. They're the evacuees I told you about."

The woman turned her head to look at them. Her eyes were the color of winter sky in her pale face. She didn't speak.

Peter walked across the room leaving damp sock prints on the floor. He held out his hand to the silent woman. "Hello. I'm Peter."

The woman stared into the space above his head. She was more ghost than person.

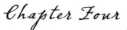

LIZZIE

MADGE POINTED TO the curved-back chairs beside the kitchen table. "Don't stand there like a couple of turnips. Sit yourselves down. It's shepherd's pie for supper."

Protecting her hands with a frayed towel, she lifted a casserole dish out of the oven and doled portions of food onto chipped china plates.

Beneath her mound of mashed potato, Lizzie found a thin layer of sludgy brown gravy with bits of onion, carrot, and turnip, but no meat; her mother always put meat in shepherd's pie. But it had been a long time since they'd eaten their potted meat sandwiches and Lizzie was ravenous, so she ate her meal.

Elsie's food congealed on her plate.

Worry lines appeared at the bridge of Madge's nose. "Not hungry, love? Never mind. I'll heat it up for you later."

She wiped her hands on the frayed towel and picked up the suitcase. "You two can wash the dishes after you've unpacked your things. First, come and see your room."

She lugged the suitcase up a steep, narrow staircase to the side of the kitchen. At the top was a tiny landing with two doors. Madge leaned her shoulder against one and shoved until it creaked open.

"Damp makes it stick," she said.

An oil lamp burned on a small table beside a narrow bed covered with a mud-colored blanket. A faded threadbare rug in the middle of the floor hid some of the yellowed linoleum. Thick blackout curtains covered the window, turning the room into a gloomy cave.

"There's only one bed," Peter said.

Madge raised an eyebrow at him. "We're not made of money. You can share with your sister. The privy's down the garden. There's a pot under the bed if you need to go at night, but you'll have to empty it yourselves."

"What's wrong with Elsie?" Peter asked. "Why didn't she talk to us? Why didn't she eat her supper?"

Madge planted her solid frame by the door and folded her arms over her chest. "There's nothing wrong with her. Elsie's my sister and I'll thank you not to gossip about her. I'm off home now. Don't forget to wash those plates."

She hurried out, leaving them alone in the drab room.

The springs squeaked when Peter bounced on the sagging bed. "Why doesn't Elsie speak?"

"I don't know," Lizzie said.

"What's wrong with her?"

"I don't know."

"Will she ever speak?"

"I don't know. And Madge said we're not to talk about it. You go downstairs while I unpack our things. It's warmer in the kitchen than it is up here."

Blustery gusts of wind sent rain tapping against the window. Lizzie shivered at the lonely sound. She unpacked the suitcase and arranged their clothes in the empty drawer of an old washstand, tucking Nana's stamps into a corner.

Sitting on the edge of the lumpy bed, she unbuckled her satchel and took out her well-thumbed copy of *The Secret Garden*. It was the story of Mary Lennox, an orphan sent from India to live with strangers in the Yorkshire countryside. Lizzie pressed the book to her chest. Just like Mary, Lizzie had been sent away from home to live with strangers. But Mary had been sent to Misselthwaite Manor, an enormous house with servants to do all the work. Lizzie had been sent to live in this small, cold, gloomy house with a woman who didn't speak.

Lizzie pulled the stiff blanket off the bed and wrapped it around her shoulders; it smelled of mothballs and dust. Surely if her mother knew just how dismal Elsie's house was, she'd come to bring them home.

Lizzie tore a sheet of paper from her notepad and laid it on the wobbly bedside table. She filled her new pen with ink and wrote:

Dear Mummy,

We have to live with a woman called Elsie. Her house is cold and the toilet's outside. I have to share a bed with Peter and it's only got one blanket. There's something wrong with Elsie. She doesn't speak. Elsie's sister Madge lives next door and she's bad-tempered. Please don't make us stay here.

Love, Lizzie xxx

After slipping her mother's letter into an envelope, Lizzie began another. She thanked her grandmother for the lovely new pen and described the long, boring train journey and the miserable walk through the pouring rain to Elsie's house. *"I don't like it here,"* she wrote. *"Please can you tell Mummy to let us come home?"*

As soon as she could, Lizzie would find a postbox and send the letters. Surely her mother would never abandon her to this miserable place.

Would she?

Chapter Five

LIZZIE

N THE MORNING, Lizzie slipped out of bed and dressed quickly in the freezing room. She drew back the blackout curtains to be greeted by cloudy skies but no rain.

Beyond the road at the front of the house, she saw a hilly field and a muddy track leading up to a farmhouse with a big stone barn. A sheep paused in its task of nibbling the grassy verge. With its jet-black head and fluffy coat, it looked as if it had stepped out of a nursery rhyme. More of the animals grazed nearby. She watched them for a few minutes, fascinated by the sight of farm animals wandering wherever they pleased.

Then she shook Peter awake. "Come and see the sheep."

He was out of bed and kneeling on the window seat in an instant. "Whose are they? Why don't they run away?"

"I suppose they belong to a farmer, but I don't know why they don't run away. Are you hungry? Let's go and see what's for breakfast."

A pan of gray, gloppy porridge bubbled on the stove. Elsie still sat in her chair, but her head lolled back and her eyes were shut.

"Hello?" Lizzie said.

Elsie didn't move.

"Should we poke her?" Peter whispered. "Is she dead?"

Lizzie shook her head. "I think she's asleep."

"Doesn't she sleep in a bed?"

"Shush! I don't know."

The back door opened, letting in a blast of chilly air. "Morning," Madge said.

She laid a gentle hand on Elsie's shoulder to wake her. She took a comb out of her pocket and tidied her sister's disheveled hair. "That's better," she said, but worried furrows scored her forehead.

She took striped bowls from a pine corner cupboard and dished up the porridge. "After breakfast you two can go out to play. But mind you don't get into mischief. Lunch is at half past eleven. If you're not here, you'll get none."

Lizzie rewound her watch and set it to the time shown by a small brass clock on the shelf over the stove. When they'd finished eating, she rinsed their bowls, laced up her shoes, fastened her coat, and followed Peter out into the back lane.

An immense valley spread out below her in a patchwork of moss and emerald green, and gold. Walls surrounding fields of irregular shapes and sizes snaked across the undulating land. In the center of the valley, a winding ribbon of trees marked the path of a river or a stream. In the distance, a thin purple smear painted the horizon where the moorland began.

Lizzie felt as if she were standing on top of the world. She had never been able to see so far — never been faced with such a vision of lush greenness. Hull was flat and crowded with streets of houses and shops, hurrying people, and noisy vehicles that belched out smelly fumes. Lizzie closed her eyes and breathed in the fresh air, savoring the earthy country smells. The only sounds were those of birds and the occasional bleating of a sheep. When she opened her eyes again, a man working in a nearby garden straightened his back and gave them a cheery wave.

Peter waved back, then bolted toward a field at the end of the lane. "Look, Lizzie! Cows!"

Lizzie peeked through the bars of a gate. A huge black-and-white cow stared back at her, its lower jaw moving from side to side. Strings of mucus dangled from its nostrils. It swished buzzing black flies away with its tail. She watched the cow, mesmerized by its chewing, but Peter wandered off up a nearby rutted track.

Lizzie followed him, scattering several browsing sheep. The track ended at a wide metal gate leading into the farmyard that she had seen from the bedroom window. Blood-red geraniums stood guard in pots by the farmhouse door. Fat golden-brown hens pecked at the ground. A duck splashed in an oblong stone trough.

A woman wearing olive-green Wellington boots, a skirt, and a blue knitted cardigan stepped out of a side door. Samuel Rosen followed her. Lizzie recognized the kind woman she'd seen in the school gymnasium.

The woman waved at them. "You must be two of the evacuees. Come on in," she called. "But mind you shut the gate, or the sheep will get in my garden."

Peter unhooked the loop of rope that held the gate closed and ran into the farmyard. Lizzie fastened the gate behind her.

"Are these friends of yours, Sam?" the woman asked Samuel.

He shook his head and looked at his feet.

Even though he'd arrived at Lizzie's school nearly a year ago, Samuel Rosen still didn't seem to have any friends, not even among the other Jewish children.

"I'm Hetty Baines," the woman said. "What are your names?"

"Lizzie and Peter Dewhurst," Lizzie answered.

"Where are you staying?" Hetty Baines asked.

Lizzie pointed toward the row of houses. "Down there with a lady called Elsie."

A brief look of concern crossed the woman's face, but then she smiled brightly and said, "Well, Lizzie and Peter, you're welcome to come and visit us whenever you want, as long as you remember to shut the gate."

She handed Samuel a bucket. "Why don't you go on over to the hen house? I'll show you how to collect the eggs in a minute." She pointed toward a small wooden shed.

Samuel turned his back on them and walked away.

Hetty Baines leaned toward Lizzie and Peter and spoke in an exaggerated whisper. "I suppose you already know he's a refugee. His teacher told me he's had a rough time. The Nazis arrested his father and burned his home so his mother sent him away. Came on a train and a boat from Germany all by himself, he did. Poor thing's only got one photograph of his family. No wonder he doesn't say much." She shook her head and hurried to catch up with Samuel.

"What's a refugee?" Peter asked.

"Someone who's been forced to leave his home," Lizzie said.

She and Peter had been forced to leave their home. In a way they were refugees like Samuel, except that they had a home they could return to one day and he didn't.

Peter ran to the gate and stood on the bottom bar. He pointed at a field. "Lizzie, come and see. There's a horse over there."

Lizzie trailed after him as he explored the farm, showing her a clump of sheep's fleece he'd pulled from a prickly thistle. He twisted the long greasy fibers into a thread before tossing them aside. "I'm hungry. Is it lunchtime yet?"

Lizzie's watch showed a quarter past eleven.

"Yes," she said, without enthusiasm.

It was Elsie, not Madge, who handed each of them a thick slice of crumbly bread smeared with a thin layer of dripping. But then she sank down into her chair as if the effort had exhausted her.

"Are you feeling poorly?" Peter asked.

Elsie didn't answer.

"Is there a postbox here?" Lizzie asked. "I've written letters for my mother and grandmother, and I'd like to send them."

"Village." It was more a breath than a word. Then Elsie scribbled something on a scrap of paper and handed it to Lizzie before leaning back and closing her eyes.

Lizzie looked at the address; it would tell her mother where to find them. She slipped the paper scrap into the envelope with her letter and stuck on one of Nana's stamps. All she had to do now was find the postbox and then wait for her mother to come.

Chapter Six

ELIJAH

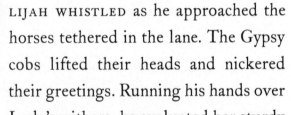

ELIJAH WHISTLED as he approached the horses tethered in the lane. The Gypsy cobs lifted their heads and nickered their greetings. Running his hands over Lady's withers, he evaluated her sturdy strength and beautiful white patches. If he sold her at Blakey Fair, he'd get a good price.

The fair was the highlight of the year. They'd park the wagons on Fair Hill and meet up with aunts, uncles, and cousins who'd been traveling in other counties for most of the summer. The streets would be crammed with horses and haggling men, and although horse trading was the main business, there'd be feasts, storytelling, music, and step danc-ing, too.

But this year the fair would be spoiled because Dad wouldn't be there, and because Elijah planned to sell Lady. Lady had been his since the day he'd helped Dad birth her. He and Lady had traveled the roads and slept beneath the stars together. Whenever Elijah hitched her to the wagon, brushed her thick mane, or sneaked her an apple, he thought of Dad. How could Elijah sell her, their best horse? How could he give the handshake and watch another man walk away with their chestnut beauty? What would Dad say when he found out?

Elijah remembered when Dad went off to join the army, so proud to be doing his duty. "I've got to do my bit, Elijah, just like everyone else. Look after yer mam and yer sisters while I'm gone. I'll be back as soon as we've sorted them Nazis out."

He wouldn't let them come to the station to wave him off. "I want to remember you in camp with the horses," he'd said.

So they'd all stood at the gate and watched him go. He'd turned at the end of the lane and waved.

Since then they hadn't heard from him and didn't even know where he'd been sent.

Elijah was the man of the family now. And if he didn't sell Lady, they'd have to take more of Bill's handouts.

Lady nudged his hand. He laid his face against her cheek and stroked her velvet nose. "I'm sorry, lass. I have to do it."

"Daydreaming again?" Bill's voice interrupted Elijah's thoughts.

Elijah's skin prickled. "I'm seeing to the horses."

"Leave them. Yer mam wants you." Bill jerked his thumb toward camp.

Elijah squared his shoulders and walked away.

Bill stuck out his good leg and tripped Elijah, sending him sprawling to the ground. "Clumsy, in't you." He smiled and limped off.

Seething, Elijah headed back to their wagon.

His mother sat on the wooden steps cuddling Rose while she fed her a bottle. Granddad Ambrose perched on a nearby log and whittled clothes pegs from alder branches.

Elijah swallowed. "Granddad, I'm going to sell Lady at the fair." The words stuck in his throat.

Granddad Ambrose put down his knife and tamped a wad of tobacco into his pipe. "You must be certain, my Elijah. If you sell her, she's gone fer good."

"I know, Granddad. But we needs the money."

His grandfather lit the pipe, scenting the air with tobacco.

Rose burped and Mammy patted her back. "We can manage without the money."

"Think on it while you check the snares fer me," Granddad Ambrose said.

"Ambrose, he can't go and check the snares. I need him to mind Rosabella. I can't tell fortunes with a babby in me arms."

"I'll take her with me," Elijah offered. "She likes a walk."

Mammy wrapped Rose in a blanket and fetched an extra quilt. She handed the baby to Elijah. "Look after her, now. Mind she comes to no harm."

Chapter Seven

ELIJAH

ITH JACK TROTTING at his heels, Elijah carried Rose through the flat meadows by the river. Her warm breath tickled his neck. When his arms began to ache, he balanced her on his hip. Skirting the village, he cut through the churchyard to the beck, then followed the little stream up the dale toward Granddad Ambrose's snares.

He stooped to pluck a flower for Rose and almost lost his balance when Bill stepped out from behind a tree. In one hand, Bill held a shovel, in the other, the neck of a sack. Something alive wriggled inside the sack, making the sides bulge and heave.

"I want you to come rabbitin' with me," Bill said.

"I can't," Elijah answered. "I've to check me granddad's snares. And besides, I've got our Rose."

"The snares are empty. I've already looked. Set the babby down. You can leave her here. We'll not be gone fer long."

Surely he couldn't mean for them to leave Rose alone. Not even Bill could be that heartless.

"I can't leave her here — she's too little!"

"You'll do as I say. Because if you don't come rabbitin' with me, I'll tell yer granddad that secret I knows about you." Bill tapped the side of his nose with his index finger.

Elijah's knees almost gave way. The secret — always the threat of the secret. That was Bill's weapon against him.

If Bill told the secret, what would Granddad Ambrose say? He'd be disappointed and angry. Would he send Elijah away? Elijah didn't want to find out.

But how could he abandon Rose?

"Mammy'll kill you if she finds out you made me leave our Rose in a field."

Bill stepped closer. He stank of stale beer and

onions. "She won't find out, because you won't tell 'er. We both knows you'll do as I say. Set the babby down. I won't say it again."

Elijah looked around in panic. There must be something he could do. Something to appease Bill. Something to keep his sister safe.

He could think of nothing.

A lone hawthorn tree stood in the center of the field.

Elijah tilted his head at the tree. "Wait while I put Rose over there."

"Be quick about it," Bill said.

Dragging his feet through the rough grass, Elijah walked slowly toward the tree. He kicked away a dried cowpat and knelt down by the trunk. Brushing away sharp bits of twig, he laid Rose on her back on Mammy's quilt and covered her with the blanket.

She smiled up at him. She was so small and helpless. He was nothing but a cringing coward for abandoning her.

He called to Bill. "Don't make me leave her here. Please let me take her back to camp. Then I'll come rabbitin' with you."

Bill's answer was a short laugh. "You'll come now. Leave her there."

Anger and misery flooded through Elijah in equal measures as he rose to his feet. Bill poked the shovel handle into his back and steered him down the field toward the beck, but Elijah hesitated on the stream bank while Bill splashed ahead through the water.

Glaring, Bill shouted at him from the far bank. "Get a move on!"

Elijah didn't bother to find a shallow place to cross. He just plowed through the water, letting it soak his trousers and boots. On the far side, he looked back toward the tree. Rose had a warm blanket. There weren't any cows in the field. She'd be all right for a while. He wouldn't be gone long.

But somewhere in the deepest part of his mind, the part that oozed superstition and dark thoughts, he knew that you couldn't abandon your baby sister and not pay a price.

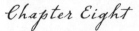

Chapter Eight

LIZZIE

LIZZIE TUCKED THE LETTERS for her mother and grandmother into her cardigan pocket. She would follow the lane, and when she got to the village, she'd ask someone where she could find the postbox.

"Where are you going?" Peter asked. "Can I come?"

She wanted to say no because he'd be a bother, but he was her responsibility now. "I'm going to post my letters. Come on."

Bright sunshine seeped from behind a cloud. A brisk breeze snapped the washing on the lines behind the houses. The air was scented with something earthy, pungent, and rich. Solid dry stone walls on either side of the lane hemmed them in as they walked, obscuring their view of the fields and moorland beyond.

Lizzie heard a mewling cry coming from the other side of the wall on her right — it sounded like an injured animal.

"Something's hurt," Peter said, standing still and cocking his head to one side.

The whimpers became louder and more insistent. Lizzie saw mossy stone steps built into the wall. She ran to the stile and clambered up. At the top, she tilted her head and listened. The ground sloped down and away from her toward a stream. She saw no animals, just a lone tree in the middle of the field.

The wind billowed her skirt and blew her hair into her eyes.

Peter tilted his chin to look up at her. "What can you see? Is it a kitten? Or a lamb? Or a baby fox?"

Suddenly, she felt impatient with him and his questions. "I can't see anything. I'll go and look. You stay here."

But as she scrambled down the worn steps on the other side of the stile, he was already climbing up behind her.

Lizzie ran, dodging prickly thistles and jumping over the dried cowpats that dotted the coarse grass. The noise grew louder and she ran faster. When she reached the tree, she stopped so suddenly that Peter almost barreled into her.

Lying on her back, on a frayed patchwork quilt, was a red-faced, bawling baby.

"*Waaa, waaa, waaa.*" The baby's little fists pounded the air. She had kicked away a knitted pink blanket, revealing a filthy mess oozing from her nappy.

Peter pinched his nose. "Eeuw! That's poo. It stinks."

The baby's cries reached a volume that Lizzie wouldn't have believed possible from something so small. Where were her parents?

"Hello?" Lizzie called. "Your baby's crying."

A blackbird trilled from the branches above them. No one else answered.

Shading her eyes, she scanned the field. "We have to find her parents." She pointed. "You look over that wall. I'll see if they're down by the beck."

While Peter ran toward the wall, Lizzie hurried to the ribbon of trees beside the stream. There was no one in the cool shade, no one paddling in the shallows, no one picnicking in the lush grasses at the water's edge — just a trampled area of mud and sloppy manure where cows had come to drink.

Lizzie ran back to the tree. The baby was crying so hard now that she couldn't catch her breath.

Peter's eyes glistened as he stood over her. "I didn't see anyone, Lizzie. What should we do?" He pressed his knuckles against his mouth.

Lizzie shut her eyes. *Think. What would Mummy do?*

"Give me your hankie."

Peter handed her a grubby square of cloth. She ran back to the beck, dipped the handkerchief in the cold water, and wrung it out.

She knelt beside the quilt in the dappled shade of the tree. Scrunching up her nose, she removed the filthy cotton rag that was wrapped around the baby's bottom. She gently cleaned the baby with Peter's handkerchief. When she'd finished, she wiped her hands on the grass.

The baby stopped crying in mid-yell. She kicked her legs, hiccupped, and reached out a chubby hand to Lizzie. She was plump and sweet with a mop of coal-black hair, huge chestnut eyes, and lush lashes like Peter's. Someone had embroidered a row of pink roses around the neck of her cardigan and the hem of her frilly pink dress.

"What should we do now?" Peter asked.

Lizzie sat back on her heels. There was no sign of the baby's family, and they couldn't just leave her. "We'll take her back to Elsie's."

Peter shook his head. "We can't take her. She's not ours."

"We can't leave her. Feel how cold she is."

He felt the baby's hands and frowned. "Where did she come from? Why is she here on her own?"

"I don't know. But she might be hungry. We'd better go."

Lizzie wrapped the baby in the blanket. Then she rolled the quilt around the dirty nappy and handed the bundle to Peter. "You carry this. I'll carry the baby."

He held the quilt at arm's length, grumbling. "It smells bad."

"Buck up. It's not far to Elsie's."

Without the dirty nappy, the baby smelled of milk and grass. Lizzie held her tight, but she was a heavy, wriggly burden, and Lizzie almost dropped her when they climbed the stile.

"Why did someone leave her in a field? Don't they want her anymore?" Peter asked.

Lizzie wondered the same thing. What kind of person would abandon a little baby in a field? Only someone horrible would do an awful thing like that.

Chapter Nine

ELIJAH

ILL LIMPED ON through meadows, hay fields, and pastures. Elijah stumbled after him, turning every few paces to look back at the field where he'd left Rose until he could no longer see the hawthorn tree. Jack trotted beside him.

They finally stopped at the foot of an egg-shaped hill topped by tall trees twisted into strange shapes by the wind. The close-cropped grass was dotted with burrows and piles of small black animal droppings.

Bill untied a string from around his waist, removed the nets looped onto it, and dropped them on the ground.

"This is Colonel Clegg's field. He dun't like us on his land," Elijah said.

"Who cares what he dun't like. Set them nets."

Elijah draped the nets over the nearest holes and pegged them in place.

Bill untied the neck of his sack and pulled out a squirming albino ferret. The jill stared at him from mean pink eyes. He stuffed her down the nearest rabbit hole, then reached into the sack and pulled out a second ferret. The cream-and-brown hob had a mask of dark fur around his glittering eyes; he was prettier than the female, but just as vicious. Bill released him into the rabbit warren.

A terrified rabbit bolted out of a burrow and straight into one of the nets. The more it struggled, the more tangled it became until Bill gripped its hind legs with one hand and its head with the other. He yanked his hands apart. *Snap.* He untangled the limp corpse and dropped it onto the ground.

Soon three dead rabbits lay side by side on the grass.

"Three's enough." Elijah fought to keep his voice even. His heart beat a tattoo of panic in his breast. He had to get back to Rose.

"I'll decide when we've enough," Bill said as he dispatched a fourth rabbit with a quick twist of its neck.

The jill poked her head out of a hole, her pink nose twitching. Bill grabbed her and dropped her in the sack. But the hob did not reappear.

Bill paced. "Got himself tucked away with a rabbit, I bet."

"I'll send Jack," Elijah said.

Kneeling beside his dog, he pointed to the warren. "Find him, boy!"

The little terrier ran back and forth, sniffing and listening. Finally he stood in one spot and stared at the ground. Elijah picked up the shovel and dug where Jack stared. A pair of inquisitive black eyes appeared in the hole. A jerking rabbit dangled from the ferret's mouth.

"Hey! You! What do you think you're doing?"

Colonel Clegg stormed through the gate at the opposite end of the field. "No poaching on my land! I'll have you arrested for this!"

Elijah pulled down his cap to hide his face. Bill yanked the twitching rabbit from the ferret's mouth and dropped it. He shoved the hob into the sack, grabbed two of the dead rabbits, and limped briskly off toward the cover of a nearby stand of trees.

"You there! Stop!" The colonel raised his gun and fired. The shot scattered a flock of crows in a flurry of squawks and flapping wings.

Abandoning the nets, the remaining rabbits, and the shovel, Elijah sprinted across the field with Jack at his heels. He vaulted the gate and ran as if the German army were after him.

If the colonel caught him, what would happen to Rose?

He couldn't be caught. He ran faster.

When he reached the cover of a willow stand beside the beck, Elijah hid and doubled over, gasping for breath. Jack panted by his feet.

Elijah parted the whippy branches and saw no sign of the colonel in pursuit. Abandoning all caution, he forded the stream and ran toward the center of the field where he'd left Rose.

When he reached the hawthorn tree, he froze, a rigid pillar of horror and fear. He did not believe what he saw.

Rose was gone.

How could she be gone?

He forced his feet to move. He circled the tree. "Rose!" he called. "Where are you? Rose!" He shouted himself hoarse.

The beck! What if she'd somehow rolled down to the water? He scoured the stream banks, oblivious to the stinging red welts the nettles raised on his arms.

Stupid! If she'd rolled away, her blanket and quilt would still be under the tree. But they were gone too.

"Where are you, Rose?" he bellowed.

But the field revealed no secrets.

Elijah clutched his stomach, doubled over, and retched. Why had he obeyed Bill?

Bill! That was it! Bill had taken Rose back to camp. He was there now, probably telling everyone how Elijah had abandoned his baby sister.

Fury built in Elijah as he sprinted back to camp. Bill would do anything to make him look bad, even if it meant putting Rose at risk. And Elijah had played right into his hands.

When Elijah arrived back at camp, he found Bill leaning against Mammy's wagon.

"Where's them rabbits? Where's me nets? Where's me shovel?" Bill said.

Elijah's shouts were frantic. "Where's Rose? What have you done with her? Is she in the wagon?"

The corners of Bill's mouth turned down. "You're the one as left her. It was up to you to fetch her back."

Elijah's mind couldn't accept the facts. Bill hadn't brought Rose back. Rose was lost. And it was Elijah's fault.

Granddad Ambrose appeared at his doorway. "What's going on?"

"It's Rose, Granddad. She's gone. I left her in a field and someone took her."

The words were inadequate — they could not convey the horror of what had happened.

The lines etched into Granddad Ambrose's forehead crinkled in confusion. "I don't understand. What do you mean?"

Fear for his sister made Elijah reckless. "Bill made me go poaching on the colonel's land. He made me leave Rose in a field up the dale. But someone took her while I was gone."

"That's a lie," Bill said. "I never made 'im leave

the babby. I found 'im idling by the beck, so I took 'im rabbitin'. Rose weren't nowhere in sight."

Blood roared in Elijah's ears. "*You're* the liar. You made me leave our Rose. You knows it."

Granddad Ambrose stepped into the space between them. "If the babby's lost, we must find her. Then we'll get to the bottom of this."

Elijah winced at the condemnation in his grandfather's eyes.

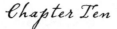

Chapter Ten

LIZZIE

LIZZIE HELD the baby close with one arm supporting her bottom and the other around her back. They'd almost reached Elsie's when a loud boom reverberated through the dale. Crows circled above a stand of misshapen trees at the top of a small hill.

"Was that a gun?" Peter asked. "Is it the Germans? Are they coming to get us?"

"If the Germans had invaded, someone would have told us," Lizzie said. "It's probably just a farmer shooting those crows."

She shifted the baby and stepped carefully around the potholes in the back lane. Peter held the back door open for her, and Lizzie stepped inside.

The sagging cushion on Elsie's chair showed the indentation of her back, but she was nowhere to be seen.

Lizzie sat down and supported the heavy baby on her legs. "Go and get Madge. I'll wait here."

"Well, I never," Madge said when she bustled in. "The lad wasn't making things up." She leaned over and took the baby from Lizzie. "This little one needs a nappy and some clean clothes."

The stairs creaked. Elsie stopped halfway down and stared. Her hair was flattened at one side as if she'd been asleep. She blinked. Then she closed her eyes and rubbed them. When she opened them again, a smile blossomed on her face.

"My little Alice is awake, then. Come to Mummy, love." She opened her arms.

Madge's ruddy face turned pale. "Oh my Lord, Elsie. This isn't your baby. She isn't Alice."

Elsie took the baby from Madge. "I'll just go and change her." She hummed a tune as she climbed the stairs.

"Has Elsie got a baby?" Peter asked.

A tiny moan escaped from Madge's lips. "Elsie's confused, love. Her mind's playing tricks on her."

She touched Lizzie's shoulder. "Go and fetch Fred. He'll be at the police station by the Coach and Horses. Take my bike. It's by the coal shed. Tell him to come home quick."

Madge's bike was big and heavy. Lizzie grasped the handlebars and pushed off. She sailed down the hills with the wind in her face and her hair flying out behind her. For the sheer joy of riding a bike, she stuck her legs out to the side and rang the rusty bell.

The ground leveled out when she passed a squat church at the edge of the village. Rows of mossy gravestones tilted like old books forgotten on a shelf. She spotted the familiar red cylinder of a postbox and rode toward it. Taking her letters from her pocket, she dropped the envelopes through the slot.

Then she wheeled the bike toward a large building with hanging baskets of orange nasturtiums, pink petunias, and bright blue lobelia dangling beside its big black doors. A painted picture of a stage-coach pulled by four strutting horses hung over the porch of the Coach and Horses pub. Next door a sign that said POLICE STATION jutted from the front wall of a house.

Lizzie leaned the bike against the wall and knocked on the door.

"Come in," boomed a voice.

The front room of the house had been turned into an office. Fred sat behind a massive oak desk, sipping tea from a blue mug. His jacket hung on the back of his chair, and his sleeves were rolled up to his elbows. Everything about him — from his barrel chest to his big smile to his huge ears protruding like dinner plates — was wide and comforting.

"Well, now, young Lizzie Dewhurst, what brings you down here?" he said.

"Madge sent me. She says you're to come quickly because I found a baby in a field."

Fred scratched his chin. "You found a baby? What kind of a baby?"

"A little girl. She was all by herself. She was crying. Elsie thinks she's a baby called Alice."

Fred thumped down his mug, sloshing tea over the rim. "Dearie me. Now we're in a pickle. I'd better go and sort this out."

"Why does Elsie think it's a baby called Alice?" Lizzie asked him.

Fred rolled down his sleeves, buttoned his cuffs, and put on his jacket. "Tell me where you found this baby."

"She was in a field down the lane from the houses. She was lying on a quilt. I shouted, but no one came. I looked down by the beck and Peter looked in the next field, but there was no one there. Why would someone leave a baby alone in a field?"

Fred didn't answer Lizzie's questions. Instead, he plunked a tall helmet over his thin hair and fastened bicycle clips around his trouser legs.

Lizzie tried again. "Why does Elsie think it's a baby called Alice?"

Fred shook his head. "It's a queer kettle of fish, that's what it is. Come on."

The two of them stepped outside, and Fred locked the door behind them.

Despite pedaling as fast as she could, Lizzie

couldn't keep up with Fred. By the time she arrived back at Elsie's, he was already installed in the kitchen with another mug of tea in his hand.

Peter stood by Fred's side holding the police helmet as if it were a precious treasure. Elsie sat in her chair, cradling the sleeping baby in her arms.

"There you are," Madge said. "Did you put my bike back where you found it?"

Lizzie nodded, out of breath from her efforts.

"Good girl, Lizzie. You were right to bring the baby back here," Fred said. "She can stay with our Elsie while I make inquiries."

"Who'd leave a baby in a field, Fred?" Madge shook her head. "It's inhuman. She could have froze to death. Or been stepped on by a cow."

"Folks do desperate things in wartime, love. There's lots of women can't manage with their men gone off to fight."

Fred took his helmet from Peter and set it back on his head. "It's odd that they'd abandon a little one all the way out here though. I'll stop at the Manor and tell the colonel what's happened. He'll want to be kept informed."

No one explained Elsie's strange behavior.

Chapter Eleven

ELIJAH

SOMEONE MUST HAVE SEEN our Rose," Granddad Ambrose said. "She didn't vanish by herself."

He sent the men to ride around the farms and the women to ask in the village. He pulled Uncle Jeremiah aside, and the two men bent their heads together. Then Uncle Jeremiah hitched up the cart and set off down the lane.

"He's gone to get yer mam. We'll wait here," Granddad Ambrose said.

Waiting was torture. Waiting left room for thoughts of carelessness, cowardice, and failure. Elijah pleaded, "Let me go and search too, Granddad."

But Granddad Ambrose shook his head. "You and me must talk."

They sat on the bottom of Mammy's steps. Elijah picked at sunshine-yellow paint flakes peeling from the wood. Granddad Ambrose fished his pipe out of his pocket and tapped it against his boot heel. "What happened with Rose?"

Elijah swallowed. "I took her with me to check the snares and Bill saw us. He said I had to go rabbitin' with him. He wouldn't let me bring Rose back to camp. He made me leave her in a field while we went to catch rabbits on the colonel's land."

Granddad Ambrose sucked in his breath. "I'd never credit Bill with abandoning a babby. Why would he do that?"

"He'd do anything to make me look bad."

Granddad Ambrose shook his head. "Bill's a rough un right enough, but he's kept an eye out fer you lot since yer dad joined the army. Why would he make you leave our Rose? And even if he did, why would you do it?"

Tell him. Tell him now.

Then there'd be no more secret and no more blackmail.

But the girl in Malton. The one Bill had seen him kiss. She was a Gorgio — one of the settled folk. Gorgios and Travelers don't mix, Granddad Ambrose always said. *Oil and water, that's what we are, my Elijah. Best we stay separate.*

Bill would see to it that Elijah was punished for kissing the girl — he might even persuade the others to shun Elijah.

So Elijah lied. "I thought Bill would hurt me bad if I didn't do what he said."

Granddad Ambrose's eyes darkened. When he spoke, his voice was brittle. "You left yer little sister alone because you were afraid of Bill? What if Rose is hurt?"

Elijah couldn't look at his grandfather.

They heard the even clopping of a horse's hooves and the rattle of a cart in the lane.

Mammy flew across the grass toward them. Her hair framed her white face in knotted tangles. She gripped Elijah's shoulders and shook him. "Where's Rose? Have you found her?"

His teeth knocked together. He shook his head, mute.

Mammy screamed. "Rosabella! My poor Rose!"

If Mammy hadn't been clutching his shoulders, Elijah would have sagged to the ground in shame.

When the searchers returned, they brought no news. Mammy took to her bed. When Elijah brought her a cup of tea, she rolled away from him and faced the wall, her back rigid with accusation. He set the tea down on the little table by the window and backed away.

At nightfall, when the small children had all been put to bed, Granddad Ambrose called a council.

The grownups sat on rickety old chairs and sturdy logs while the older children stood in the darkness behind their parents. The fire crackled, spitting sparks into the night air. The smell of tobacco mingled with the smell of wood smoke. Flames lit the circle of anxious, weary faces. Only Mammy was missing.

Elijah paced, wearing a path between their wagon and the fire.

Granddad Ambrose, his face ashen with worry, cleared his throat. "No one's found our Rose. We'll search again at dawn tomorrer."

"What about Ephraim?" Uncle Jeremiah said. "Should we send word to him?"

Elijah shuddered. Not Dad. Dad would never forgive him.

"Nay. It would take too long, and he's enough on his plate with learning the army's ways," Granddad Ambrose said.

"What about the fair?" someone asked. "Blakey Fair's the biggest of the year and we've horses to sell."

"Jeremiah and Lilah and their bairns will stay with me and Vi and Elijah and the girls. We'll look fer Rose," Granddad Ambrose said. "The rest of you can leave fer the fair in the morning. We'll catch up with you after we find the babby. Does anyone have owt to say about that?"

Elijah stepped into the center of the circle. He felt eyes boring into him, judging him. He licked his dry lips and said, "If everyone goes to the fair, there won't be enough of us left to look fer Rose."

"We'll make do," Granddad Ambrose said.

But how could so few of them search all the nearby villages and farms?

"We'll need help, Granddad. We could ask the police."

A chorus of rumbling dissent erupted around the

fire. Granddad Ambrose shook his head. "Police'll not help us. You know that."

Elijah hung his head. Of course it was a stupid idea. But he was desperate or he'd never have suggested it.

"Fool!" Bill said. "The police'd sooner arrest us as look at us." He turned toward Granddad Ambrose. "I've no horses to sell. I'll stay here with you and search fer the babby."

Bill lived for the fair; he thrived on the gambling and the money he got for his fiddle playing. He'd miss the biggest fair of the year only if he were dead or had something important to gain.

"It's settled, then." Granddad Ambrose looked at each member of the group for confirmation.

A log collapsed into the fire in a heap of hissing embers. Bill stood and pointed an accusing finger at Elijah. "I've summat to say about 'im. He couldn't even look after his sister. His mam's beside herself in there." He jerked his thumb at Mammy's wagon. "He's a disgrace. I say we shun 'im to teach 'im a lesson."

Elijah tensed. Surely they wouldn't make him an

outcast — banish him from his home and everything he loved.

Yet his deepest, darkest thoughts told him that exile was the punishment he deserved for deserting his sister.

Granddad Ambrose pushed himself up off his log seat. He straightened his back and thrust out his chin. His voice was sharp, his eyes narrowed and hard. "There'll be no talk of shunning. The lost babby is punishment enough fer the lad."

Bill looked away from Granddad Ambrose. If he was disappointed, he didn't show it.

The rest of the group scattered to pack and prepare for travel. Elijah retreated to the patch of grass beneath Mammy's wagon. He curled up beside Jack, too miserable to care about the damp chill.

Elijah woke to the warbling trill of a thrush and the first faint smudge of dawn lighting the sky. Along with the awful memory of losing Rose came the realization that he'd forgotten about Lady — today she'd leave for the fair. He rubbed some warmth back into his stiff legs and set off for the lane.

Lady was tethered on the grass beside the road. He wound his hands in her thick mane and laid his face against her cheek.

"I've made a mess of things, lass."

She nuzzled him, blowing her warm breath onto his neck.

"I'll miss you, but I have to sell you."

A boulder filled his throat. Dad wouldn't want him to sell Lady. She was the best horse they'd ever had.

But Dad wasn't here. It was up to Elijah to make the decision. He unfastened the rope that tethered her.

Chapter Twelve

LIZZIE

IZZIE SAT on the garden wall and tucked her skirt beneath her legs to protect them from the rough stones.

Peter perched next to her and kicked his heels against the wall. "Is that baby Elsie's?"

"I don't think so," Lizzie said.

The baby's cries had woken her in the night, and she had lain awake, wondering, *Why does Elsie think the baby is hers? How could anyone mistake someone else's baby for her own?*

"Didn't the baby's mummy want her?" Peter asked.

"I don't know."

Lizzie remembered her own mother's sorrow

when she and Peter boarded the bus that would drive them away from home. She thought of all the other sad-faced parents who'd had to say goodbye to their children. Hadn't whoever left the baby been sad to walk away from her?

Peter poked his elbow into her side, interrupting her thoughts. "I'm going to see the pig."

He jumped off the wall, opened the gate, and hopped down the uneven garden path. Lizzie followed him past neat rows of onions, carrots, and runner beans to a low brick building at the bottom of the garden.

An enormous pig lay on his side on a pile of straw in a pen outside the building. When he saw them, he flapped his ears and struggled to his feet. His small eyes disappeared into folds of pink flesh.

Peter reached between the bars of the pen and scratched the pig's hairy snout. "Hello, boy."

"Don't do that. He might bite."

"He won't. I'm going to call him Curly."

"You can't. He's not yours."

Peter knit his eyebrows into a scowl. "You're just cross 'cos you didn't think of it first."

"Giving a pig a name is silly."

Peter turned away and kicked at a clod of earth. The back of his scrawny neck had a ring of dirt above his grimy collar.

Lizzie sighed; she was supposed to be looking after him, not being mean to him.

She patted his back. "Sorry. Curly's a good name for him."

The sharp crack of a cricket bat hitting a ball came from the lane behind them, followed by excited shouts. Lizzie and Peter turned to watch the game. The batter ran between wickets as the bowler stamped his foot in exasperation.

"Do you think they'll let me play?" Peter said.

"Go and ask," Lizzie replied.

As soon as Peter was installed as a fielder at the far end of the lane, Lizzie sneaked away. She walked to the field where she'd found the baby and circled the tree. Something shiny glinted in the long grass. Lizzie bent down, parted the clump, and found a brass horseshoe, about the size of her palm, attached to a red ribbon.

It was too big and heavy to be a necklace, but it

could be a baby's toy. Was it a clue? Lizzie tucked the horseshoe into her pocket and set off to show it to Fred.

As she walked through the village, she noticed a handwritten sign in the window of the shop:

LOCAL BOY JOINS UP.
ANOTHER LAD TO MAKE
US PROUD.

Lizzie pressed her nose against the glass and squinted at the newspaper on the top of the pile beneath the sign. It showed a photograph of a smiling young man waving from a train window. The man's uniform made Lizzie think of her father; it had been so strange to see Daddy dressed in khaki instead of his usual work suit.

Where was he now?

Adolf Hitler had started the war by sending his army to invade Poland, but Poland was far away and no British soldiers had been sent to fight there — at least that's what Lizzie's mother had told her. So surely Daddy was safe. But if Hitler decided he wanted to take other countries as well as Poland, then Daddy might be sent over the sea to fight.

And if Hitler decided to invade England, then no one would be safe!

Lizzie turned away from the window and its unwelcome reminders of the war. She saw Fred standing by the village green with a thin woman and walked toward them.

The woman's stringy gray hair framed a face that was all jutting edges and sharp corners. "That field they're camped in is full of rubbish, and their horse droppings foul the road," she said to Fred. "Those Gypsies are a disgrace. And why aren't their men in the army like our boys?"

Fred clasped his hands behind his back and rocked on his heels. "They've been helping Bert Baines with his potatoes. I daresay they'll be off to the Blakey horse fair soon, and then they'll not trouble us."

"Bert should know better," the woman continued. "They never do a decent day's work. They're common thieves. I've had to keep my door locked ever since they arrived. Betty Arkright says they're looking for a lost baby. How on earth did they lose a baby? They're irresponsible."

Lizzie fingered the horseshoe in her pocket. The Gypsies had lost a baby? It must be the baby she had found!

She looked up at Fred, expecting him to have the same thought, but Fred showed no reaction. Instead, he inclined his head at Lizzie. "This here's one of our evacuees. Lizzie, say hello to Mrs. Sidebottom."

Lizzie sucked in the giggle that fought to escape at the sound of the funny name. "Hello, Mrs. Sidebottom."

"That's another thing, Fred. How long are these evacuees staying? The one I've got is eating me out of house and home."

"Have a heart, Ethel. They're just little nippers sent away from their parents. The least we can do is feed them up."

Mrs. Sidebottom gave Fred a curt nod, straightened the carnations in her basket, and scurried off toward the church.

Fred pushed back his helmet and wiped his forehead with a huge handkerchief. "Ethel Sidebottom never has a kind word to say about anyone. Come on, Lizzie. I could do with a cup of tea after that."

Lizzie perched on the edge of a straight-backed chair in the police station. She wanted to ask Fred about the lost Gypsy baby, to see whether he thought it was the baby she'd found, but she waited while he pushed a pile of papers to the side of his desk and took half of an oblong loaf out of a breadbox. He spread a thin layer of butter onto the cut end of the bread, held the loaf in place against his chest, and carved off a slice. He handed it to Lizzie along with a pickled onion and a cube of cheese.

Lizzie nibbled the crusty bread and crumbly cheese, saving the vinegary onion until last. Pickled onions were her favorite — Daddy's, too.

"Petrol's been rationed, and now they say food will be rationed too," Fred said. "Enjoy it while you can, lass — we might have to manage without soon enough. But I can do without butter and cheese if it'll help our lads in the army." He chewed thoughtfully.

"That lady said the Gypsies were looking for a baby," Lizzie said. "Do you think it's the baby I found?"

Fred paused. "It could be. Ethel Sidebottom's not the only one who's told me about a lost Gypsy baby."

"Why does Elsie think it's a baby called Alice?" Lizzie asked.

"That's nothing for you to worry about," Fred said, screwing the top back on to the pickled onion jar.

Lizzie fished the horseshoe out of her pocket. "I went back to the field where we found the baby and this was in the grass. I think it belongs to the baby. I think it's a clue."

Fred fingered the shiny object. "It's a horse brass. The Gypsies hang them on their horses' harnesses. It's supposed to bring good luck."

"Then she must be a Gypsy baby! Will you look for her family?" Lizzie asked.

Fred paused. "If them Gypsies left that sweet little thing in a field, they don't deserve to keep her. They've got too many little ones as it is. She'll be better off with our Elsie instead of being dragged around the country in all weathers with that lot, but I'll see what the colonel says about it."

"What does the colonel have to do with it?"

"He's our magistrate. He enforces the local law — acts like a judge, you might say."

Fred wrapped the ribbon around the horseshoe and stowed the little bundle away in his trouser pocket. "You'd best run along now. I've got work to do."

Lizzie walked slowly back through the village. Grownups made all the decisions for children. Grownups had decided that the baby should stay with Elsie. Grownups had decided that children should be evacuated to the country to live with strangers.

But what if the baby would rather go home than stay with Elsie? What if Lizzie and Peter would rather face the bombs than live with strangers?

Chapter Thirteen

LIZZIE

IZZIE STOPPED at the old stone bridge. Leaning over the mossy parapet, she stared down into the fast-flowing river. Water weeds trailed in long streamers, wafting with the current. A few small fish darted into the sandy shallows.

Pow! Pow! Pow! A rowdy gang of boys raced across the grassy oval of the village green aiming crude wooden guns at one another and imitating the sound of gunshots.

A tall, freckle-faced boy at the head of the group skidded to a halt. His red hair was shaved high on the sides of his head revealing a scalp the color of

Elsie's pig. "I'm bored of this game. Let's go and see them Gypos instead," he shouted at the others.

The boy ran past Lizzie and over the bridge with the rest of his gang in hot pursuit.

Except for the rag-and-bone man who drove his horse and cart down their street and the woman who came to their door selling clothes pegs, Lizzie had never seen Gypsies. She was curious, so she followed the boys along the wide path by the river. They stopped and huddled in the shadow of a hedge beside a barred gate. Hiding behind the wide trunk of an oak tree, Lizzie peeked through a gap in the tangled bushes.

She saw a row of Gypsy wagons parked in a field beside the river. Most of the wagons looked like wooden carts with curved green canvas tents fitted on top. But one wagon, parked separately from the others, had fancy carved wooden sides and bright yellow steps leading up to a red door decorated with paintings of horses. Smoke billowed out of a chimney poking up through the roof.

Despite their unusual homes, the Gypsies themselves didn't look very different from anyone else in Swainedale. A woman wearing a pinafore over her cotton dress gathered blackened cooking pots from the ashes of a fire and tied them to the back of a wagon. A sun-browned man with shirtsleeves rolled up to his elbows and a bright blue scarf knotted around his neck led a beautiful horse past Lizzie's hiding place. The horse had splashes of brown over its white body, feathery hair dangling over its hooves, and a luxurious long tail.

A small rock sailed through the air, startling Lizzie. The rock landed on the ground behind the horse's hind feet, but neither the horse nor the man noticed the missile.

Lizzie turned and saw the red-haired boy poke another boy in the chest. "You throw like a sissy. Watch me."

He picked up a chunk of gray rock, hefted its weight, and lobbed it into the field. The rock smacked into the nearest wagon with a dull thud.

A girl collecting washing from a hedge pointed and shouted something that Lizzie didn't understand.

"They can't even speak proper English," the red-haired boy said.

Then the gang of boys hurled a volley of rocks into the field before running past Lizzie, hooting with glee. A woman, her face screwed into a mask of fury, shook her fist at their retreating backs.

Shocked, Lizzie bobbed down behind a thick part of the hedge. Lots of people didn't like Gypsies. But throwing stones at them! That was a horrible thing to do.

As the boys disappeared into the distance, the Gypsies continued with their tasks. Several men hitched brown- and black-splashed horses to five of the nine wagons. Then an old man wearing a wrinkled three-piece suit and a flat cap held the gate open while the wagons rumbled and creaked out of the field.

Men drove three little metal carts pulled by three of the spotted horses while other horses were led away by teenage boys. Lizzie had never seen so many horses in one place before.

The Gypsy women and children walked silently beside the wagons to the clattering accompaniment of the horses' hooves on the road.

The Gypsies were leaving. Did that mean the baby wasn't theirs after all? Or was Fred right to think that they didn't want her?

But not everyone left. When the old man closed the gate, four wagons remained in the field.

Lizzie stood up, slowly straightening her stiff legs, just as a lean boy with wavy black hair crawled out from beneath the fancy wagon. He walked toward her, his eyes locking on hers and his face creasing in anger.

In panic, Lizzie backed away, turned, and sprinted toward the bridge and away from the rage in his dark eyes.

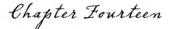

Chapter Fourteen

LIZZIE

L IZZIE RAN all the way back to Elsie's.

"Any later and you'd have got no lunch," Madge said, handing her a slice of bread and a hard-boiled egg.

She spoke her next words softly. "I want a word with you two before Elsie comes down." She cast an anxious glance up the stairs. "It's about the baby. You're not to tell anyone where you found her. You're to say she's an evacuee that came on the train with you."

Peter's eyes were as round as an owl's. "But that's not true. Mummy says we're not supposed to tell lies."

"Peter . . ." Lizzie shook her head at him, trying to stop him from making Madge angry.

Madge responded by putting her hands on her wide hips. "Well, now. You're not afraid to say what you think, are you?"

Peter never seemed to get into trouble.

Madge leaned toward him, bringing her face close to his as if sharing a secret with him. "That baby makes our Elsie smile. She hasn't done that in a long while. Whoever abandoned the little one didn't want her. The baby's better off with Elsie, so a little white lie won't harm anyone."

The baby did make Elsie smile. And Lizzie had seen most of the Gypsies leaving. If they didn't want the baby, then why shouldn't Elsie keep her?

"We won't tell where we found the baby," Lizzie promised.

"Good girl. I knew you had some common sense," Madge said.

"Well, I can't stand around here all day chatting — I've got things to do. Remember what I said: Mum's the word." Madge tapped her finger against her lips and then hurried out the door.

"We can't tell lies. Mummy would be cross,"

Peter said. He put his thumb in his mouth and sucked on it.

"We have to do what Madge says now, not Mummy." But Lizzie sounded more confident than she felt.

Elsie appeared and navigated the steep stairs with the whimpering baby cradled in her arms. She had dressed the little girl in a pink knitted pram suit and pixie hat. "I'm going to take Alice for a walk to settle her down. You two can come if you want. Lizzie, can you hold her for a minute while I put on my coat?"

While Elsie buttoned her coat, Lizzie cradled the fussy baby. The little girl stopped crying, reached up a tiny hand, touched Lizzie's cheek, and gurgled.

"She likes you," Elsie said, smiling. "You're a natural with her."

But when Elsie laid the baby in the big blue pram and covered her with a blanket, the baby began to cry again.

Outside, dreary gray skies and a damp chill greeted them. Leaden clouds hung low over the moors. Elsie raised the pram hood and fastened it in place.

The springs squeaked as Elsie pushed the pram

down the lane, but the movement soothed the fussing baby. Soon she slept, looking like a fat, fuzzy caterpillar in her cocoon of blankets.

Peter hung back and whacked at roadside plants with a stick.

A woman and two small girls approached from the direction of the village. The woman wore a shapeless dark skirt and a short jacket. A flowered scarf covered her hair, and she carried a big basket over one arm.

"Gypsies!" Elsie frowned. "Those girls will be full of germs." She pulled the corner of a blanket over the sleeping baby's head and pushed the pram to one side of the lane, leaving the Gypsies room to pass.

But the woman stopped. The little girls clutched at her skirt.

"Pardon me, missus. Is that yer babby?" the woman said.

"Of course she's my baby." Elsie gripped the pram handle and leaned in as if to continue down the lane, but the woman blocked her way.

"Little uns are a blessing. Care to buy a ribbon

fer yer precious?" The woman lifted a red ribbon from her basket.

Elsie shook her head, but the woman was persistent. "Let's have a look at yer little un? Then I'll know what color suits her. I'll even give you a ribbon fer free." She leaned over the pram and reached out a thin hand.

"Don't touch her!" Elsie's voice was sharp.

The woman grabbed at the blanket. "Just a quick look."

Elsie slapped her hand away. "Get away from her." She spat the words. Then she spun the pram around, running it over the woman's feet, and turned back up the lane.

Elsie's angry actions and the fury in her voice shocked Lizzie.

The Gypsy woman trembled. Her lips were a thin white line. Her eyes were soft pools of velvet darkness drowning in sadness. One of her little girls began to cry.

The woman clutched Lizzie's arm. "Someone took me babby yesterday. I'm looking fer her. Can you help me?"

A large raindrop plopped onto Lizzie's nose. More fell on her head. Shivery prickles ran down her spine.

This must be the baby's mother. Should Lizzie tell her about finding a baby in the field? Or should she keep her promise and the secret?

The Gypsy's eyes blazed with a sudden determined intensity. "If that woman's got me babby, there'll be trouble."

Lizzie yanked her arm from the woman's grasp and turned to get Peter, but he was nowhere in sight.

Chapter Fifteen

ELIJAH

AMP WAS QUIET, like a country church-yard. Elijah couldn't bear the silence without Lady and Rose. He whistled for Jack and set off up the lane. Someone knew where his sister was; he had to find that someone. He'd start with the field where he'd left Rose. Maybe whoever took her had left a clue there.

When he arrived, he found a small boy wearing a lopsided school cap and a pair of very muddy shoes standing beneath the hawthorn tree.

"Who are you?" the boy asked. "Is that your dog? I like him. What's his name? Where do you live?"

His clear-eyed enthusiasm was infectious, and

Elijah smiled in spite of himself. "His name's Jack. We're camped down by the river. Where do you live?"

"In Hull. But we were sent here 'cos of the bombs. My daddy's in the army. He's going to fight the Germans. Is yours?"

Elijah nodded. "Me dad's in the army too. If you're not living at home, where are you staying now?"

The boy pointed at the row of stone houses. "Over there with Elsie."

A flurry of raindrops spattered their heads. Elijah turned up his collar. He kept his voice light. "Have you heard owt about a babby found in this field?"

Two small lines appeared between the boy's eyebrows. He looked worried, as if he wasn't sure what to say. "Do you mean a baby? It's a secret. I'm not s'posed to . . ."

"Peter!" A girl stood on the top of the stile by the lane. Frizzy tendrils of hair framed her thin face. Stick legs poked out from beneath her knee-length skirt. "We have to go back to Elsie's," she called. "It's raining."

"That's my sister. I have to go," the boy said, and ran off across the field.

Elijah called after him, "Wait. What about the babby?"

But the boy was already climbing the rough stone steps, the girl reaching down to help him up.

Something about her tangle of hair jogged Elijah's memory. Wasn't she the girl he'd seen lurking near the hedge by camp? Was she another of the Gorgio stone-throwers who tormented them? Or had she been spying on them? The boy had looked almost guilty when Elijah asked about a baby. Did they know something about Rose?

He'd have to catch up with them to find out.

Elijah sprinted across the field and scrambled over the stile, but instead of the two Gorgio children, he found Mammy standing in the lane. Angela and May huddled against her skirt, shivering in the rain.

"Mammy? It's pouring. What are you doing here?"

"There were a woman in the lane just now. She had a babby in a pram. She wouldn't let me look. It were our Rose. I know it were."

"How do you know it were Rose?"

"I felt it here." Mammy pummeled her fist against her chest. Wet tendrils of hair escaped from her sodden scarf, but she didn't seem to notice the rain.

"Where did the woman go?" Elijah asked.

Mammy stabbed a finger at the houses. "Up there."

A familiar shape materialized out of the rain ahead of them. Duchess slowed to a lumbering halt, and Granddad Ambrose looked down at them from her back. The wool of his jacket was dark with rain. Droplets dripped from the brim of his cap.

"What's going on?" he asked.

"Mammy says she saw a woman with our Rose."

"She was in a pram, Ambrose. The woman wouldn't let me look at her, but it were Rose, I'd bet me life on it." Mammy pointed up the lane. "The woman went up yonder."

Hope swelled in Elijah. Mammy had a sixth sense; if she said the baby was Rose, it was Rose.

"If the babby's with that woman, she's more than likely safe and dry fer now, but these little uns is froze." Granddad Ambrose tipped his head at Angela and May. "We must get them back to camp."

"You and Mammy can take them. I'll find Rose."
Elijah would not, could not, leave her again, not if
she was this close.

"Nay, lad. These people won't open their doors
to a Gypsy in this weather. We'll wait until the rain
stops."

"But, Granddad..."

"Folks 'round here are suspicious of us as it is,
my Elijah. We can't barge in and make trouble. We'll
talk with the others and decide what to do."

Elijah hoisted Angela and May up onto
Duchess's broad back. He walked beside Mammy
with his head down against the wind and rain. But
now he had hope. Now he knew Rose was near. He
would get her back. He just needed a plan.

Chapter Sixteen

LIZZIE

LIZZIE FOUND A TOWEL for Peter's dripping hair. "You shouldn't disappear like that. I didn't know where you'd gone." She paused. "That boy looked like one of the Gypsies. What did you say to him?"

She bent down and whispered into his ear, "You didn't say anything about the baby, did you?"

He mumbled into his chest. "I didn't tell the secret."

Elsie rocked in her chair, cuddling the sleeping baby. "Madge has some wellies for you two. You'd better go and get them, Lizzie. You'll need them if this keeps up." She nodded her head at the rain-streaked window.

Lizzie ran to Madge's house and knocked on the door.

"Come in out of the rain. I expect you've come for these." Madge pointed to two pairs of olive-green boots on the floor by the sink.

Madge's kitchen was cozier than Elsie's, with a big rug on the flagstone floor and flowered curtains at the window. On a shelf above the stove, Lizzie saw three silver-framed photographs. In one, a young woman wearing a sundress reclined in a deck chair.

"That's our Susan when we went to Scarborough," Madge said. "She came home when her young man joined the air force. She's lucky to be working for the colonel now."

"What does she do there?" Lizzie asked.

"She helps him with his paperwork and such. He's a very busy man these days, what with his Local Defense Volunteer work on top of everything else. He says he couldn't manage without her." Madge beamed with pride. "I expect you'll see her at the weekend — she gets Saturdays and Sundays off."

In the second photograph, a woman wearing a floaty dress danced with a man whose long coattails streamed out behind him.

Madge followed Lizzie's gaze. "That's me and Fred. Dancing in Harrogate."

Lizzie leaned in for a closer look. The man was a younger, slimmer version of Fred, but it was hard to believe that the glamorous woman, with her hair slicked back in waves, was Madge.

"You wouldn't know it to look at us now, but we was good. We even won some competitions." Madge's voice had a wistful edge.

"You look like a film star," Lizzie said.

Madge's smile smoothed out all the angry little creases around her lips.

In the last photograph, a man had his arm around a laughing woman, who held a chubby baby.

"That's Elsie," Lizzie blurted. "Whose baby is she holding?"

Madge straightened the shiny frame. "You might as well know. It's Alice, Elsie's baby. She died last year of the double pneumonia. And then Norman, Elsie's husband, was killed in an accident with a tractor. Elsie's not been the same since."

Elsie's baby, Alice, had died — that was the secret! But how could Elsie think this new baby was Alice?

"Doesn't Elsie know the baby we found isn't Alice?" Lizzie asked.

Madge sighed. "Her mind's playing tricks on her. She sees what she wants to see."

Lizzie thought about Colin Craven in *The Secret Garden*. He was lonely and sad because his mother had died and his father ignored him. He believed he had a lump on his back even though his spine was perfectly straight, and he was sure he'd die young. Colin imagined things because he was miserable. Elsie must be lonely and sad too — was that why her mind played tricks on her? Was that why she thought the lost baby was Alice?

"Madge, *we* know the baby's not Alice. How can Elsie keep her?"

Madge set her mouth in a firm line. "Listen to me. Now that our Elsie's got this baby, she's more like her old self. If we give the baby up, she'll be un-happy again."

Lizzie twisted a lock of hair around her finger. "We saw a Gypsy in the lane. She was looking for a lost baby. What if the baby is hers?"

"Humph! No one leaves a baby in a field by accident. Those Gypsies aren't natural mothers. They don't take proper care of their children. There's not a one can read and write. None of them goes to school. They run around all day, filthy dirty most of them."

The Gypsy children Lizzie had seen in the camp didn't look neglected, but leaving a baby in a field certainly wasn't taking proper care of it.

Madge continued. "The colonel says Elsie can keep the baby. So that's what we'll do, and you'll not say a word to anyone about finding her in that field. Not even to your own parents. Do you understand?"

Lizzie nodded her agreement. What else could she do?

The Gypsy woman stalked Lizzie's dreams that night.

When Lizzie woke the next morning, she stared at the cracks that crisscrossed the bedroom ceiling. Surely the baby would want to be with her real family; Lizzie would give anything to be with hers.

If she helped the baby, she'd be going against Madge and Fred. But if she didn't help the baby, no one else would.

Folding back the blanket, Lizzie crept out of bed

and dressed quietly without disturbing Peter. She sneaked down the stairs and out of the house.

The colonel had said Elsie could keep the baby, so Lizzie would have to change the colonel's mind — Madge and Fred would never argue with him. But Lizzie didn't know where he lived, so she walked into the village, hoping to find someone to ask.

A woman cycled up to the shop, leaned her bike against the wall, and unlocked the door.

"Excuse me," Lizzie said. "Can you tell me where the colonel lives?"

"The colonel's a busy man. What do you want with him?" the woman said.

Lizzie thought fast. "Fred Arbuthnot, the policeman, sent me."

"Oh, well, then," the woman said. "You can't miss the Manor — it's the biggest house in the village. Just keep going along the road."

The colonel's house was so big, it had a chimney at each end of the roof. Lizzie walked through the huge iron gates and down the curved gravel driveway toward the massive oak door. Back at Elsie's, her plan had seemed simple. But now that she was outside the grand house, nothing seemed simple.

What if the colonel chided her for interfering? What if Susan found out about her visit and told Madge? What if Fred discovered her lie?

There's no sense in worrying about something until it happens, Nana would say.

Instead of knocking on the imposing front door, Lizzie followed a narrow flagstone path around the back of the house. Beyond an archway in a tall brick wall, rows of vegetables and ranks of apple trees marched in straight lines like soldiers.

The gardens were so like those she imagined at Misselthwaite Manor in *The Secret Garden* that Lizzie half expected to see Ben Weatherstaff weeding the plants while a cheeky little robin watched him.

Instead, a harsh voice behind her made her spin around. "Where do you think you're going?"

Lizzie recognized the man who'd met them at the railway station when they'd arrived in Swainedale. The colonel repositioned his round glasses on the bridge of his nose and peered at her; his eyes were huge, distorted by the thick lenses.

Before her courage failed her, Lizzie plunged into her story. "I've come about the baby I found in a field. You told Fred that Elsie could keep her, but the Gypsies are looking for a baby. Shouldn't we find out if she's their lost baby?" Her words tumbled out in a rush.

The colonel arched an eyebrow over the black frame of his glasses. "Impertinent child — questioning my decision. Those Gypsies are poachers and thieves. They don't deserve to have children, especially not one they left in a field. Now run along."

The gravel crunched under his feet as he turned and strode away.

Lizzie watched his retreating back. She had disobeyed Madge to come here, and the colonel hadn't even given a minute's consideration to her request. She had not helped the baby. And if the colonel told Fred about her visit, she would be in trouble.

There was only one thing left to do.

Chapter Seventeen

ELIJAH

ELIJAH SHIVERED in the chill morning air. Mammy handed him a slab of bread and a bottle of cold tea. He winced at the sight of her pale face and bloodshot eyes. She spoke to the space above his head.

"I'm going to see if I can find that woman we saw yesterday. I'll take Angela and May. Yer granddad's gone off on Duchess. He says you're to stay here in case there's news of Rose."

"I can't stay. Not again. I want to look fer Rose meself."

"Do as yer granddad says." She walked away, leaving him standing alone in the field.

Elijah grabbed the ax and began chopping the logs in the pile that Bert Baines had given them, taking out his frustration on the firewood. The hard work calmed him. He stopped to rest, wiping sweat from his brow with his handkerchief.

A girl approached the gate. Her too-big boots smacked against her bare legs with each step she took. He recognized the frizzy hair, the pinched face, and the mouth that seemed too small for her teeth. She'd been to their camp before.

Planting his feet, he folded his arms over his chest. "What do you want? Have you come to throw stones?"

She flinched and Elijah paused. She was the sister of the boy he'd met in the field. If he was rough, he wouldn't find out what they knew about Rose.

He swallowed his impatience and gentled his voice. "Sorry. That's what folks like you generally do when they comes here." He opened the gate and stepped forward. "I'm Elijah. What's yer name?"

"Lizzie." She looked at the almost-empty field. "Where did the others go?"

What was it to her?

But he bit back his retort. "They're off to the fair. We had to stay here because me babby sister is lost."

She stared at him for so long that he felt the telltale heat of a blush beginning in his ears and spreading to his neck.

"How did you lose a baby?" she finally asked.

She was left by a stupid cowardly fool, he thought.

"She were left by accident, and someone took her."

"Who leaves a baby by accident?" Her voice, pitched high anyway, rose even higher.

She was like a terrier with a rat — not letting the questions go. Why was she being so nosy?

"Do you know summat?" he asked. "If you've seen our babby, you should tell me now."

He took a step toward her.

She opened her mouth but shut it again without saying anything. She turned away from him as if she were going to leave, but then she didn't move. She didn't seem to know what to do.

"Why did you come here?" Elijah said.

"Someone told me you lost a baby. I came, I came..."

She looked over his shoulder, and he saw her

eyes widening with fear. "I have to go," she said, and suddenly ran off down the lane.

Elijah turned to see what might have frightened her.

Bill stood by his wagon with a pair of headless chickens dangling from one hand and his knife clutched in the other. He was staring up the lane in the direction the girl had taken.

Elijah beat his clenched fist against his thigh. Bill was like a bad penny, turning up at all the wrong moments. He'd frightened the girl — Elijah was certain she knew something — but now she'd run away and Elijah couldn't follow her because Bill would see.

Elijah needed to leave camp so that he could make his own decisions, and he had to get away from Bill. Then he could look for the girl.

He sprinted to Mammy's wagon and stuffed a handful of potatoes into his jacket pocket. He grabbed a canvas sheet and tucked it under his arm, then he whistled for Jack and ran out of the gate. Cutting across fields, he began the climb up the dale side, pushing through knee-high bracken. When he reached the flat moorland, he followed a sheep path through the thick heather. Just a few weeks ago, heather flowers had carpeted the moorland in vivid purple, and he'd carried Rose up to see them; but now the flowers had faded to brown, and Rose was gone.

Crossing a boggy patch of moorland, he jumped from one clump of marsh grass to another in a futile attempt to keep his boots dry. He passed the old stone cross standing sentinel over the wild land and leaped over a tiny beck. By the time he reached one of Colonel Clegg's grouse-shooting blinds, he was breathless.

Heather plants sprouted from gaps between the mossy stones in the blind's low wall, providing perfect camouflage. From here, Elijah could see for miles in all directions; no one could sneak up on him. Best of all, he was directly above the Baineses' farm and the row of houses.

He didn't know how long it would take to find Rose, so he built a shelter. He draped the brown canvas sheet over the top of the blind and anchored it with rocks. He unsheathed his knife and gathered an armful of bracken fronds to spread over the damp floor.

When his shelter was finished, he set off down the dale side to the houses. They were close to where he'd left Rose. That's where he'd start looking for the girl.

Chapter Eighteen

LIZZIE

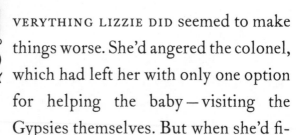

EVERYTHING LIZZIE DID seemed to make things worse. She'd angered the colonel, which had left her with only one option for helping the baby — visiting the Gypsies themselves. But when she'd finally plucked up enough courage to go to their camp, she'd run away from the Gypsy boy without telling him anything.

The boy had been gruff and unfriendly, and the big man with the bloody chickens had frightened her. What if all the Gypsies were rough and wild like those two? What if the baby wouldn't be safe with them? She knew so little about the Gypsies — how could she decide what to do?

As she walked through the village she saw a new sign in the shop window:

GOVERNMENT SAYS WE'RE
IN FOR A LONG WAR.
RATIONING COMING SOON.

How long was a long war? Would it be weeks or months? Would the war last until Christmas? She couldn't imagine being away from home for that long.

Lizzie sat on a bench by the village green, leaned forward with her elbows on her knees, and rested her chin on her hands. At least she could try to help the baby. But how? She was afraid to go back to the Gypsy camp.

She remembered the kind lady at the farm: Hetty Baines. Mrs. Baines had soft plump curves and a smile that reminded Lizzie of Nana. Nana couldn't help Lizzie now, but if Lizzie told Mrs. Baines the truth about the baby, would Mrs. Baines know what to do? Or would telling her cause even more trouble?

Lizzie walked at a snail's pace back up the lane. She stopped to sniff tall spears of bright pink flowers blooming in the grassy verge. Standing perfectly still, she watched a tiny wren flitting between branches in the hedge. She dawdled, postponing the moment when she would reach Elsie's house and have to make a decision about what to do next.

When she finally reached the row of houses, she stopped walking. A woman hung washing on a line at the back of the nearest house while a group of small boys played marbles in the lane. Lizzie took a deep breath and then continued on and up the track leading to the Baineses' farm. Lifting the loop of rope, she opened the gate, before closing it behind her.

But it wasn't Mrs. Baines she met; it was the Gypsy boy Elijah.

He stepped out from behind the barn and blocked her way. His hair was unkempt, and dirt crusted the bottom of his trousers. Mud caked his little dog. Lizzie imagined Dickon, Mary Lennox's friend, to be brown and earthy, as if he'd sprung from the land, but this boy seemed a creature of dank, dark places.

"I want to talk to you," he demanded.

How had he arrived at the farm before her? Either he knew a shortcut, or she'd taken longer to walk up the lane than she'd thought. She wanted to get away from him, but something vulnerable about his expression kept her standing there.

"I have to find me sister. It's my fault she's lost." His desperate voice was a stark contrast to his wild appearance.

"If you don't help me, none of the folks 'round here will. I've got to find our Rose. Mammy's right sad without her. We all are. Will you help me?" He held out his hands, pleading with her.

Lizzie cast a quick glance at the farmhouse. She was close enough to shout for help.

"You have to answer some questions first," she said. "You said you'd lost your baby sister. What does she look like?"

Elijah's eyes softened. "Our Rose has black hair and bonny brown eyes and dimples in her cheeks. She's little. She can't even crawl yet. She'd a dress and a knitted coat and a blanket, too."

The lost baby's clothes had roses embroidered on them. Roses for Rose?

"How did you lose her?"

A door slammed somewhere nearby, and they both jumped. Lizzie thought she saw a face at one of the farmhouse windows.

Elijah turned his head to scan the farmyard. "Too many people can see us here. Come 'round the back of the barn. We'll be hidden from plain sight there, and I can tell you everything."

Lizzie shook her head.

"I won't hurt you," he said. "I promise. Come on."

Her mind said, *Don't go!* But her feet followed him to the barn.

Patches of bright orange lichen made a pretty contrast to the weathered gray stones of the barn wall. Lizzie stood beside a wooden door that had been made in two pieces — the top half was open as if waiting for a horse to peer out, but the bottom half was closed. A skinny black cat slunk toward them but darted away when it saw Elijah's dog.

Elijah spoke fast. "Bill, that man you saw at our camp, made me leave our Rose in a field. Then someone took her."

"How did he make you leave her?"

Elijah didn't flinch from her question. "He forced me go rabbitin' with him. I wasn't gone long, but when I got back to the field, Rose were gone."

Lizzie had to be certain. "Did she have a toy?"

"Aye. A little brass horseshoe on a ribbon."

"Oh." Lizzie covered her mouth with her hand.

Elijah changed in an instant, like the weather when a sudden squall blows in from the sea. His face hardened. His voice was harsh. "You know summat about our Rose. I know you do. Where is she? You'd better tell me. Now!"

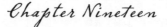

ELIJAH

LIZZIE SHRANK BACK against the barn wall. He'd frightened her again! She was his one link with Rose, and somehow he kept on scaring her. He was suddenly conscious of his uncombed hair and filthy clothes. He must look wild — no wonder she was afraid of him. What could he say to convince her to help him?

"I'm sorry," he said, stepping away from her. "I don't mean to be rough with you. It's just that I'm fair desperate to find me sister. I wouldn't ask fer help if I didn't have to."

He'd never ask a Gorgio for help if he could avoid it, but now he'd no choice.

They stared at each other. It was Jack who moved first. He sniffed Lizzie's feet, then licked her hand.

Good boy, Elijah thought. *Make friends with her.*

She stooped to pat Jack's head. "Why should I help you?"

"Because no one else will."

She frowned at that, but then she straightened her back and looked him in the eye. "Do you love your sister?"

What kind of silly question was that? "Of course I do."

"Then why did you leave her?"

His shoulders slumped. "I gave in to a bully, and I'm right ashamed of that. Our Rose has suffered fer it. I need to get her back. Do you know where she is?"

A rooster crowed in the farmyard. Somewhere nearby a horse whinnied. Elijah waited for her answer.

Lizzie spoke so quietly that he had to lean toward her to hear what she said. "I'm the one who took your sister from the field. I heard her crying and she was all by herself, so I took her to Elsie's. I didn't know what else to do."

"Who's Elsie?" he asked.

"She's the person I'm staying with. She had a baby who died. A little girl called Alice. Now Elsie thinks your sister is Alice."

Elijah's knees almost gave way beneath him. "That woman must be mad if she can't tell the difference. I can't leave our Rose with no madwoman. I've got to get her now."

"You can't," Lizzie said. "I'll get in trouble. Fred and Madge and the colonel all say that Elsie should keep the baby."

The words exploded from him. "Mammy's right about you lot. You think you can do anything. You're all rotten. No Gypsy would steal a babby from her family."

She jutted her chin at him. "We're not all rotten. And if you hadn't left your sister in that field, none of this would have happened."

It was a punch to his stomach. "You're right. It is my fault. But I've got to get Rose back. Please help me."

The sharp planes of her face softened. "All right. I'll help you."

Hope coursed through him, but a low growl rumbled in Jack's throat.

"Someone's coming," Elijah said, and peered around the corner of the barn.

Bill slid off his horse by the gate. He tied the horse to a post, smoothed his jacket, and limped toward the farm.

What was he doing here?

"Who is it?" Lizzie whispered.

"Bill. The one as made me leave our Rose."

Bill rapped on the farmhouse door with his knuckles. When Hetty Baines opened it, he removed his cap and clasped it in his hands. Hetty Baines folded her arms across her chest and frowned at him.

Elijah strained to listen but caught only a few words of the conversation.

Bill twirled his cap as he spoke. "... boy ... trouble ... good-fer-nothing ... thief."

Hetty Baines shook her head. "Not Elijah ... Ambrose ... good lad."

Lizzie poked Elijah's shoulder. "What's happening?"

"Shh!" he said. "Let me listen."

But the conversation ended abruptly when Bill gestured at the barn. Hetty Baines shook her head again, more vigorously this time, and pointed down the track before closing the door. Bill crammed his cap back onto his head and limped back to his horse. He led the animal through the gate, then looked back over his shoulder as he fastened the loop of rope.

The scrawny green-eyed cat chose that moment to dart across the farmyard. Jack pointed his ears and gave chase. Lizzie reached out to grab him, but the little dog was too fast and pursued the cat around the back of the hen house.

Bill stared at the barn.

Elijah shrank behind the cover of the wall. Had Bill seen Jack? If Bill returned and found Elijah with Lizzie, there'd be more trouble.

"I've got to get our Rose," Elijah told Lizzy. "I've got to get her back home. Quick! Show me where she is."

"How are you going to get her away from Elsie?" Lizzie asked. "You can't just rush in. Fred's a policeman. If he sees you, he could arrest you."

Hold yer horses, Elijah. That's what Granddad

Ambrose said whenever Elijah was impatient. *Think on it first.*

Lizzie was right — he couldn't just barge in and grab Rose. He needed to think and plan.

"Come with me up to the moor," he said. "We'll be safe up there — you can see fer miles so no one can sneak up on us. Please come and help me find a way to rescue Rose."

Chapter Twenty

LIZZIE

IZZIE STOOD at the corner of the barn and risked a quick look into the farmyard. She saw the big Gypsy heaving himself up onto his horse. If she went straight back to Elsie's, she might meet him on the track or the road. And, anyway, Elijah and his baby sister needed her help, and she did want to see the moorland.

"I'll come with you," she said.

"We can't walk on the road — Bill might see us," Elijah told her. "We'll have to climb up the hill. Can you manage it?"

She looked where he pointed. The hillside was steep and uneven, crisscrossed by narrow sheep paths cutting through the thick bracken. Fortunately, she was wearing her wellies — her shoes would have been useless in the mud.

"I can manage."

Elijah led her up the dale side, following one of the sheep paths. His movements were quick and fluid, as if he was born to run over this wild land. Bracken fronds so tall they almost reached her waist brushed against Lizzie's legs and tripped her. She felt clumsy beside Elijah.

"Keep low," he said as he stopped to look toward the lane. "I can't see where Bill's gone."

Elijah's clothes blended with the colors of the hillside, but Lizzie's bright red cardigan was a stark contrast to the greens and browns around her. She tried to crouch as she walked.

A small brown-streaked bird tweeted at them from a prickly bush. Lizzie tilted her head to listen.

"Yon's a meadow pipit," Elijah said. "There's lots of them 'round here. Pretty little things, they are."

Lizzie thought of Mary Lennox's friend Dickon, who befriended the wild creatures. She smiled. Elijah liked wild things just like Dickon.

As they climbed higher up the dale side, Lizzie lagged behind Elijah. She was panting and thirsty by the time she reached the top.

Below her, the dale stretched for miles in a patchwork quilt of fields. Miniature animals, like toys in a farm set, dotted the land. Pencil scribbles of smoke drifted up from cottage chimneys. But up on the moor, there wasn't a single dwelling or tree, just a vast windswept expanse of empty land.

"Look." Elijah pointed. "Bill's gone back to camp. We're safe fer a while."

Far away a tiny horse walked down the lane toward the village.

In the distance to Lizzie's right, something tall jutted from the ground. They followed a narrow path toward it through the rough heather. She saw that it was a cross made from big rectangular blocks of pitted gray stone placed on top of each other.

"Why is there a cross up here?" she asked Elijah.

"Granddad says the monks put it here to guide pilgrims across the moor to the abbey," he said. "The abbey burned down, but the cross is still here."

Lizzie looked out across the bleak landscape

— wherever the pilgrims came from, they must have had a long, lonely walk to the abbey.

Elijah climbed up the stepped base of the cross, shaded his eyes with his hand, and peered out over the moorland.

"There's no one around," he said. "And we can see if anyone comes up the road."

He sat down on the top step and leaned against the cross. Lizzie sat beside him. The wind tousled her hair and lifted her skirt, but the sun-warmed stone offered some shelter.

"We have to make a plan," Elijah said. "Does that woman ever leave Rose on her own?"

Lizzie shook her head. She struggled to think of something that would make Elsie leave the baby alone. Then the seeds of an idea sprouted.

"Elsie's got a pig," she said.

"Lots of people 'round here have pigs," Elijah said.

Lizzie told him her idea.

"That's a grand plan! Let's go and do it," Elijah said.

"We can't go now. We'll have to wait until tomorrow morning when Fred's at work and Madge has gone down to the shop."

Elijah chewed a stalk of grass as he considered what she'd said. "I don't want to wait another day, but I've no plan to beat yours. We'll do it. It's a grand idea, Lizzie."

Warmth crept up Lizzie's neck and into her cheeks. Elijah sat so close that she felt the heat of his body. She slid along the step to make a gap between them.

Elijah's little dog barked at a fat brown bird hiding in the heather.

"Leave it," Elijah said, and the dog lay down at his feet.

"What kind of bird was that?" Lizzie asked as it hop-flew away.

"Grouse. The colonel owns all this land. Him and his fancy friends come up to shoot them."

It was such a pretty bird with its bright red eye stripes. "It's wrong to shoot wild things," Lizzie said.

Elijah snorted. "Grouse is good eating. And shooting's good sport — to the colonel, anyway."

"It's wicked to shoot birds for sport," Lizzie said.

Dickon would never kill a pretty grouse, not for sport or food.

Elijah just shrugged. He slipped his arms out of his jacket and held it out to her. "Here. You look cold."

She draped the heavy jacket over her shoulders. The coarse wool was itchy and smelled like wet grass mixed with sweat.

"Listen," he said, cocking his head to one side. "The wind sounds like lost bairns crying fer their mams."

"Wuthering." That was the word they used to describe the howling of the wind at Misselthwaite Hall in *The Secret Garden*. It was a good word for such a lonely lost sound. Lizzie pulled the jacket tighter around her.

"Rose is a Traveler like me. She belongs out here in the wind and the wild," Elijah said, flinging his arms out wide. "Not shut up in some stone house where she can't see the sky and the stars."

"But what about when it's cold and rainy?" Lizzie asked.

"Our wagon's cozy, and there's always a fire and summat hot to warm us up."

"Why do you move around so much? Why don't you live in one place?"

"We go where there's work. In the summer, that's in the fields," Elijah told her.

"But how can you go to school if you're always moving around?" She sounded like Peter — asking too many questions. But she wanted to know what life was like for Elijah and his little sister.

He tensed and spoke bitterly. "We don't go to school because if we do, Gorgio children pick on us. And they're not the only ones — the teachers pick on us too."

Lizzie remembered the stone-throwing boys. "Why don't the people in the village like Gypsies?"

"No one likes us. Gorgios, settled folk like you, say we're thieves. But plenty of Gorgios is thieves. I've worked many a day and not been paid what I were promised."

Lizzie looked down at the houses. "I'm sorry people are so mean to you."

She stood and handed him his jacket. "I'd better go now. Elsie will be wondering where I am. Meet me behind the pigsty tomorrow. I'll be there after breakfast."

Chapter Twenty-One

LIZZIE

 HE ROAD SNAKED down the dale side in a series of zigzag loops. While Lizzie walked down it, she had to lean backwards to keep her balance on the steepest parts.

She thought about what Elijah had told her. What would it be like if everyone you met disliked or even hated you? She wondered where he'd go and what he'd do while he waited to rescue his sister.

She arrived back at Elsie's house at the same time as Peter.

"I've been playing with Sam," he said. "He showed me where the hens hide their eggs. We found four."

"That sounds like fun," Lizzie said.

Peter chattered on while he unlaced his shoes. "Sam's been riding on a horse, that lucky duck. He said he'll ask Mrs. Baines if I can have a go."

Sam was Lizzie's age. She was curious about why he'd want to spend time with a seven-year-old boy. But Peter was kind and he wouldn't tease Sam about his German accent like some of the other boys at school had done.

Elsie tiptoed down the creaky stairs. "Don't make a noise you two — Alice is sleeping." She reached into her apron pocket. "This came while you were out."

Mummy's neat handwriting marched across the envelope. Lizzie took the letter and ran upstairs to read it in the privacy of the bedroom.

Peter followed her to the chilly room. Lizzie drew the blackout curtain to one side and climbed onto the window seat, scrunching up against the whitewashed wall to make room for her brother. Sliding her finger into one side of the envelope, she tore it open and pulled out the letter, savoring the faint whiff of lavender.

"Read it out loud, please," Peter said.

Dear Lizzie and Peter,

How are you both? Have you settled in? Do you know which school you'll be going to yet?

School! So much had happened since they'd arrived in Swainedale that Lizzie hadn't even thought about going to school.

There haven't been any bombs yet, thank goodness. I've had a letter from Daddy. He's been marching a lot and he says he's a crack shot now, but the army food is terrible! Nana's moved in with me to keep me company, and we're growing lettuce on top of the bomb shelter. Nana's knitted three balaclavas and two scarves for our brave soldier boys.

Lizzie folded her arms over her chest to squeeze away the sudden wave of homesickness.

I miss you so much. It's very quiet here without you.

Love and kisses, Mummy

"I'm starving. I'm going to tell Elsie about the letter and see if she's got anything to eat," Peter said.

Mummy hadn't mentioned Lizzie's letter — she must not have received it yet. Lizzie took her pen and notepad out of her satchel, pushed the lamp on the bedside table to one side, and began to write.

Dear Mummy,

Elsie is kind, but Madge is bossy. I'm trying to be good and look after Peter.

A blob of ink splotched from the pen nib. Lizzie dabbed it with a sheet of blotting paper.

I found a lost baby in a field. She was all alone and she was crying, so I brought her back to Elsie's. Elsie had a baby called Alice but Alice died. And Elsie's husband died too. Now Elsie thinks the baby we found is Alice.

Lizzie hadn't meant to tell her mother about the baby, but the minute she began to write, the words poured out.

The baby's a Gypsy and her family wants her back. But Madge and Fred say the baby's better off with Elsie. Colonel Clegg says so too. They made me promise not to tell anyone where I found the baby so Elsie can keep her. Isn't that kidnapping?

Stealing. Kidnapping. Whatever you called it, surely it was wrong.

Madge is cross with me because I want to give the baby back. I don't know what to do.

Love, Lizzie

She folded the letter, slipped it into her dress pocket, and curled up on the window seat.

The baby cried in the next room, softly at first and then becoming more insistent.

Lizzie heard Elsie push open the door and comfort the little girl. "There, there. Don't fret. Mummy's here."

Elsie brought the baby in to Lizzie. "Was it a letter from home?"

Lizzie nodded. "Mummy says she misses us."

"Of course she does. And you must miss her too."
Elsie smiled sympathetically. "How would you like
to hold our Alice while I get the supper ready?"

The baby reached up to grasp a strand of Lizzie's
hair. Lizzie kissed the top of her head. To help Elijah
and this sweet little bundle, she would have to betray
Elsie. How could she do that?

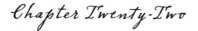

Chapter Twenty-Two

LIZZIE

THE NEXT DAY, threatening steel-gray clouds blanketed the dale. Rivers of rainwater gushed from the drainpipes, creating puddles the size of small ponds. Wind battered the windows and sent dustbin lids clanging down the back lane.

The awful weather kept everyone inside, and Lizzie could not put her plan for the pig into action. Instead, she stared out the window at the bleak rain-soaked landscape and thought about Elijah. Had he gone home? Or was he out in the wild weather somewhere?

She wondered if it was raining in Hull. At home on a day like this, Daddy speared slices of bread on a long-pronged fork and toasted them over the fire. Mummy made hot sweet cocoa, and they all did jigsaw puzzles and read stories together. But Lizzie's parents were far away now, and Elsie didn't have cocoa or jigsaw puzzles or even any books.

Elsie's newspaper lay on the kitchen table and Lizzie picked it up. On the first page, above a photograph of a scowling Adolf Hitler, were big black letters:

WANTED FOR MURDER

Lizzie scrutinized the ugly face with its staring eyes and blocky black mustache. Adolf Hitler was the chancellor of Germany. *His* army had invaded Poland. *His* soldiers had destroyed the shops and homes of the German Jews. *His* actions had forced children like herself, Peter, and Sam to leave their families. How was it possible that one man could cause so much fear and suffering?

She set the newspaper down. Elsie fetched a ball of wool and some needles, and Lizzie cast on enough stitches to make a scarf. Remembering what Nana had taught her, she made alternate knit and purl stitches across the row until her needles became tangled with her thumbs. She held the knitting out to Elsie. "I've dropped a stitch, and I don't know how to pick it back up again."

"I'm not much good at it, I'm afraid," Elsie said. "But I'll try. Here, you hold Alice."

Lizzie took the baby and watched Elsie struggle with the knitting — Nana would have been able to sort it out in a jiffy. Lizzie cuddled the baby and sang nursery rhymes to her while Peter cut pictures from an old magazine with a blunt pair of scissors. The little girl wriggled, drooling over a white teething ring, and Lizzie wondered whether a baby could be homesick. Did this one miss her real family, or was she happy here with Elsie, Lizzie, and Peter?

The back door burst open. Madge blew in with one hand holding down her skirt and the other gripping her dripping umbrella. She stood with her feet apart, oblivious to the puddle growing on the floor.

"Lizzie, come over to our house for a minute." Her voice was flint hard.

Elsie looked up from the knitting. "Is everything all right?"

Madge nodded. "I've something for Lizzie, that's all. It's at our house."

After handing the baby back to Elsie, Lizzie followed Madge through the rain and worried. Had the colonel told of her visit? Had Susan said something? Had someone seen her with Elijah?

Madge took a crumpled piece of paper from her pocket and shook it in Lizzie's face. "Explain this!"

Fear washed over Lizzie. She saw her own handwriting, her own notepaper, her own letter!

Madge waved the paper at Lizzie. "I found this in your pocket when Elsie brought me your clothes to wash. What do you have to say for yourself?"

Lizzie spoke through chattering teeth. "That's private. You shouldn't have read it."

Madge puffed out her chest like an angry rooster. "After all we've done for you, this is how you repay us? I said you weren't to tell anyone about finding that baby!"

"You can't steal a baby!" The words burst from Lizzie.

"What did you say?"

Lizzie lifted her chin. Anger chased the fear away.

"You shouldn't make us tell lies. And you shouldn't steal that baby! It's a horrible thing to do."

"And you should mind your elders and betters."

Madge ripped the paper into tiny squares and dropped them into the stove. "There'll be no more letters unless I read them first. It's bad enough that we have to put up with strangers in our homes, without them causing a packet of trouble."

Elsie was waiting for Lizzie by the back door. "Is something the matter?"

Lizzie pushed past her, ran upstairs, and banged the bedroom door closed. She threw herself onto the bed and pummeled her fists into the pillow. She hated this miserable, miserable place.

The bottom of the door scraped against the floor as Peter pushed it open. He peeked around the edge. "Elsie sent me to see what was the matter. Are you crying?"

"No," Lizzie said, and wiped her sleeve across her face.

He walked over to the bed. "You look like you're crying. Are you sad 'cos we can't go home?"

"Aren't you?" Lizzie asked.

He nodded. "I want to see Mummy and Daddy."

"Me too. But Daddy's in the army now, so we can't see him."

Peter stuck his thumb in his mouth. He looked small, forlorn, and lonely — just the way Lizzie felt. She pulled him onto the bed and put her arms around him. The relentless wind and rain beat against the window. If only they could go home and leave all the problems behind, but they were trapped here in Swainedale.

Chapter Twenty-Three

ELIJAH

RAIN POUNDED on the canvas above Elijah's head. A blustery wind blew damp chilly gusts through the open entrance to his shelter. He huddled against Jack for warmth and chewed raw potatoes to quell his hunger. He thought of Rose hemmed in by walls and a roof — a prisoner in the stone house until he could rescue her.

As long as Lizzie kept her promise.

He'd have to trust Lizzie; he'd no choice, but trusting a Gorgio — he'd never thought he'd resort to that.

· · ·

Rain kept him imprisoned in the grouse blind for a day and a night, but the next morning, golden spears of hopeful sunlight streaked a blush-pink sky. Everything looked fresh and clean, even the sheep.

He crawled out of the shelter, stretched his cramped limbs, and squelched through the boggy mud. Today he would rescue Rose, whether Lizzie helped him or not.

"Stay close," he told Jack. "And mind you keeps quiet."

As furtive as a cat on the prowl, he followed the sheep paths through the heather and bracken, skirted the Baineses' farm, and then crossed open fields toward the neat gardens behind the houses.

He smelled the rank stench of pig coming from a brick building about halfway along the row of gardens. After squeezing into a gap behind the sty, he squatted down and waited.

The sun burned the early morning dew off the grass and made the steaming pig manure stink. Elijah shifted position, releasing a flood of pins and needles into his numb feet. Where was Lizzie?

Jack pricked up his ears and thumped his tail.

Elijah held his finger against his lips. "No barking."

"Elijah?" Lizzie's exaggerated whisper came from the other side of the pigsty.

He peered around the corner. "I'm 'round the back."

Her hair was pulled into a tight ponytail, making her face look thinner than ever. The skin beneath her red-rimmed eyes was the color of a faint bruise.

"What's wrong?" he asked. "You haven't changed yer mind, have you?"

"Of course not." She rubbed at her eyes, leaving a smear of dirt across her cheek. "Madge didn't go to the village today. She's in the house. Do you think we should wait another day?"

"Not bloomin' likely. I won't wait a minute longer to get Rose back. We'll do it now."

He unlatched the gate to the pen. Then he pulled a leafy carrot from a nearby row and waved it at the pig. "Come on, piggy, piggy. Come and get it."

The pig planted his front trotters on the ground and pushed himself up. He yanked the carrot from Elijah's hand and devoured the treasure with a greedy snuffle. Then he peered at the open gate with his beady eyes. With a surprising burst of speed, he galloped into the garden, trampling carrot tops as he went.

The pig rooted up potatoes, stripped tender green pods from the runner beans, and tugged at the turnips. Soon the garden was strewn with the wreckage of Fred's vegetables.

Lizzie gaped at the sudden devastation. "I'll get Elsie before he ruins anything else. You hide in the coal shed." She pointed to a single-story whitewashed addition at the back of the house.

When Elijah pulled the door shut behind him, the darkness inside the coal shed was absolute — a dense clinging thing that pressed on his eyes and interfered with his balance. He stumbled against a mound of lumpy coal. Jack snuffled and wheezed beside him.

Elijah heard a woman's voice right outside the shed. "Oh, my Lord! What a mess!"

He hardly dared breathe.

A door creaked. A different woman spoke. "What's going on, Elsie?"

"The pig's out, Madge. He's in Fred's garden."

Coal dust tickled Elijah's nostrils. He twitched his nose. "*Schnzzzzz!*"

He pinched his nostrils and held his breath.

A flurry of sneezes erupted outside the shed. "*Atchoo! Atchoo! Atchoo!*" Then Lizzie's voice. "I think I'm catching a cold. I'm sorry, Madge. It's my fault the pig got out. I tried to stop him, but he ran away."

"You should be more careful. Whatever will Fred say?"

Their voices faded. Elijah counted to a hundred before he opened the door a crack.

All clear! He and Jack ran into the house.

A pile of nappies teetered on the kitchen table. Rose's horseshoe lay beside them. Elijah stuffed it into his pocket, thrilling at its familiar cool curves. A narrow staircase led upstairs. Was Rose up there? Or was she in the room at the front of the house — the one behind the closed door?

He heard a soft chortle. Abandoning all caution, Elijah opened the door into the front room.

Lizzie's brother stood beside a blue pram. And in that pram sat Rose. She opened her arms to Elijah and smiled the most delicious smile he had ever seen. Elijah's heart melted in a river of molten joy.

The boy squinted at him. "I've seen you before. Why are you here?"

Every nerve in Elijah's body told him to grab Rose and run. But he coaxed his mouth into a smile and spoke quietly. "Lizzie sent me. She said you're to come and help catch the pig."

The boy put a protective hand on the side of the pram. "I'm not s'posed to leave Alice."

Elijah edged closer to him "The missus said you could leave . . . Alice . . . with me." His tongue tripped on the unfamiliar name.

"Oh, goody," the boy said. "I want to chase Curly too." He ran through the kitchen and out the back door.

With trembling fingers, Elijah unbuckled the harness holding Rose in the pram. He pressed her to his chest and stroked the soft skin on the back of her neck. "You're safe now."

Then he ran.

Chapter Twenty-Four

LIZZIE

THE PIG LOWERED his snout and munched his way along a row of floppy turnip tops.

"Shoo! Get away from there." Madge flapped her hands. "You go 'round the other side, Elsie. Make sure he doesn't get past you."

Madge poked the pillaging pig with a broom. "You daft bugger, get in that sty!"

The pig squealed once and complied.

Madge shut the gate and tugged on the latch to make sure it was secure. She dabbed her face with her apron. "I'll enjoy every bite of that animal."

Squashed plants, half-eaten turnips, and chewed carrots littered the ground. "I'm sorry I didn't latch the gate properly," Lizzie said. She felt like a traitor.

"Don't worry, pet. You didn't do it on purpose," Elsie said, pressing a loose plant back into the soil with her heel.

But Lizzie had done it on purpose.

Peter met them at the garden gate. Disappointment clouded his face. "Did you catch Curly already? The boy said I could help you."

Elsie frowned. "What boy?"

Peter looked as if he'd been caught sneaking a biscuit from the tin. "He said he'd look after Alice while I helped you catch Curly."

Elsie shoved Peter out of her way and barged through the back door. Her harsh scream sliced through the quiet. "Noooooooooooo!"

Madge hurried into the house. Lizzie and Peter followed.

In the front room, Elsie scrabbled through the bedding in the pram. She heaved the blankets and mattress onto the floor. Then she tore the cushions from the sofa and tossed them aside, knocking a china bowl off a table. The bowl shattered on the floor in a shower of pottery shards.

They watched, speechless, as Elsie ripped the

blackout curtains from the rods and upended the overstuffed armchair.

Finally, with the room in shambles around her, Elsie sank to her knees and wailed — a thin, wretched, heart-piercing sound.

Peter stuffed his knuckles into his mouth and pressed up against Lizzie. Shaking, Lizzie put her arm around his shoulders.

Madge knelt beside Elsie and held one of her hands. "What's happened, love? Where's Alice?"

"Gone. She's gone."

Madge grabbed the side of the pram and pulled herself up. She faced Lizzie, her expression chiseled from stone. "You've got something to do with this. Where's the baby?"

Lizzie shrank away from her. "I don't know."

That was true; she didn't know where Elijah had taken his sister.

Elsie stood. Ignoring them all, she walked out the front door.

"Wait! Elsie, where are you going?" Madge hurried after her. But she stopped at the door long enough to glare at Lizzie. "I'll deal with you later, when we've found Alice."

Lizzie had never dreamed they'd go after the baby; that wasn't part of the plan. If they found Elijah's family, what would they do? Would Madge try to take the baby back?

Lizzie took Peter's hand and pulled him out of the house. Ahead of them, Madge half walked, half ran down the lane beside Elsie.

Lizzie heard the squeak of Fred's bike before she saw him riding over the crest of the hill. He stopped when he saw Elsie and Madge, and lowered his foot to the ground.

"What's going on?" he asked, puzzled.

Elsie paid no attention to him as she continued on down the lane. Her apron strings trailed behind her like streamers as she hurried toward the village.

"What's up with Elsie? Where's Alice?" Fred asked Madge.

Madge jerked her head at Lizzie. "Ask her."

Lizzie gripped Peter's hand. "The baby's gone back home. Her brother came for her."

"How do you know that?" Fred asked.

Lizzie looked into his kind eyes. "Because I helped him."

Chapter Twenty-Five

ELIJAH

ELIJAH TUCKED ROSE into his jacket and held her tight against his chest. She reached up, pulled his nose, and giggled. He thrilled at the weight of her bouncing against him as he ran back home. His feet flew over the ground.

He paused at the edge of camp, savoring the moment. Granddad Ambrose sat on his steps, oiling the chain of a bike while Angela draped damp clothes over the hedge to dry.

Elijah grinned and stepped into view.

Angela's earsplitting screech startled a crow from his perch in a nearby tree. "Mammy! Elijah's got Rose!"

Granddad Ambrose's head snapped up. Angela's yell brought Mammy out onto their porch. An onion fell from her hand and bounced down the steps, rolling to a stop in the long grass. She leaped off the steps and ran across the meadow, her loose hair flying around her face.

Lifting Rose from Elijah's arms, Mammy covered her in a storm of kisses. "Oh, Rose, my Rose."

Rose buried her chubby hand in Mammy's tangle of hair and snuggled her face into Mammy's neck. Elijah drank in their happiness.

Granddad Ambrose's smile was so wide that his pipe fell out of his mouth. He hugged Elijah and thumped him between the shoulder blades. "Kushti, lad. Kushti."

As the girls and Granddad Ambrose gathered around Mammy and Rose, Bill watched them from beside his wagon.

A voice from behind interrupted their celebration. "Alice!"

Elijah whipped his head around. A wisp of a woman stood by the gate.

"Alice," she said again, and hurried toward them with her eyes fixed on Rose.

Mammy pointed an accusing finger. "You're the woman had me babby in that pram. You *stole* our Rose."

Angry exclamations from Elijah's family peppered the air. Elijah moved to stand between Mammy and the woman.

"Elsie!" The village policeman leaned his bike against the gate and strode into camp as if he were the lord of them all. "Elsie, this is no place for you."

He took the woman's arm, but she shook him off. She never took her eyes off Rose, not even when Lizzie, her brother, and a second woman arrived.

The policeman pointed at Rose. "That baby is a ward of the court. Hand her over immediately."

Granddad Ambrose faced the huge man. "The babby's me granddaughter. We'll not hand her over!"

"That baby was abandoned, and whoever stole her from our care was trespassing. Those are criminal offenses," the policeman said.

Mammy glowered at him. "She were lost, not abandoned. What right do you have to take her from us?"

The policeman clasped his hands behind his back. "The right of the law."

Lizzie stepped forward. "Rose is their baby, Fred." She looked up at him. "You can't take her away from her real family. It's wrong."

Lizzie's words hung in the air. No one spoke.

The wispy woman blinked and stared at Lizzie. Then she reached out a hand as if to touch Rose. Mammy recoiled and moved away from her.

"I think I knew she wasn't Alice right from the start." The woman's voice cracked. "Losing a child is the worst pain there is." She looked at Mammy. "I'm sorry."

Longing and loss were written in the lines on her face. Elijah should have hated her, but he felt only pity as the woman turned and walked out of the field.

The policeman looked down and brushed imaginary fluff from the front of his jacket. Then he cleared his throat and spoke to Granddad Ambrose. "I want your lot gone by tomorrow. Clear off and don't come back. You're not welcome here."

The other woman grabbed Lizzie's brother's hand and said, "Come along."

"What about Alice?" he asked.

"She's staying here," the woman said, and dragged him through the gate.

Lizzie, her face pale and pinched, watched them leave. She stood alone, looking miserable.

Elijah gently took her hand. "Come and meet me family. They'll want to thank you."

He led her to his grandfather. "Granddad, this is Lizzie. She's the one as found our Rose and helped me get her back."

Granddad Ambrose clasped Lizzie's hand. "We're grateful to you, lass."

Mammy nodded in agreement.

But then Bill limped toward them. "It's time you heard what the lad's been up to, Ambrose. This un's another of his Gorgio lasses. He collects them every place he goes. He's a wrong un."

Before Elijah could object to Bill's accusation, Granddad Ambrose said, "We'll settle this bad blood between you two once and fer all. We'll have a council, and the girl can join us."

He spoke to Lizzie. "There's been trouble twixt Bill and Elijah, and mebbe you can help us find the truth of it. Will you sit with us fer a spell?" He pointed to a lopsided wooden chair by the burned-out fire.

Hugging her arms to her chest, Lizzie sat on the chair. Uncle Jeremiah and Aunt Lilah perched on other chairs by the fire pit while Elijah's cousins stood behind them, arranged in order of height. Mammy sat on a log and cuddled Rose while Elijah stood on one side of Granddad Ambrose and Bill stood on the other.

"Elijah speaks first," Granddad Ambrose said.

Bill scowled.

"I took Rose with me when I went to check the snares, but Bill stopped us in a field by the beck. He said I had to leave Rose behind and go rabbitin' with him."

Mammy leaned forward and focused her eyes on Elijah, as if she could search out the truth. He thrust back his shoulders and stood upright under her scrutiny.

"Bill found out a secret about me, summat I didn't want you all to know. He kept on threatening to tell it. I shouldn't have left our Rose in yon field, but I were scared he'd say what he knew."

Elijah faced Granddad Ambrose.

"When we was in Malton, I used to meet a girl there, a Gorgio. Bill saw me with her." Elijah looked at his feet — if he saw disappointment, or worse, reflected on his grandfather's face, he'd never be able to finish. He spoke in a rush, running the words together as if saying them fast would make them sting less. "Bill said you'd shun me fer going with one of the settled folk. He said you'd send me packing, and now that me dad's gone, he could have Mammy fer himself."

Bill shook his head. "You can't believe a word the boy says."

Angry lines creased Granddad Ambrose's forehead. "Did you do owt to be ashamed of with this girl?"

Elijah swallowed and answered. "No, Granddad. I kissed her once, that were all."

His grandfather's face softened. "Foolish lad, we'd never shun you fer one kiss."

Relief flooded through Elijah. But Mammy looked up at Bill. "Did you make Elijah leave our Rose in that field?"

"The lad's lyin' to you, Vi. He dun't want to get in trouble fer meeting this girl." He jerked his head at

Lizzie. "I bet *she's* the reason he left the babby in the first place."

Granddad Ambrose held out his hand. "That's enough. We'll hear what the girl has to say."

Chapter Twenty-Six

LIZZIE

BILL GLOWERED AT LIZZIE, but Elijah's grandfather spoke gently. "We'd take it kindly if you'd tell us how you found our Rose."

Lizzie ran her tongue over her dry lips. She explained how she'd heard something crying in a field. She told how she'd gone to investigate the sound and been shocked to find a baby instead of the animal she'd expected. "The baby was all alone and she was crying. She was cold, so I took her to Elsie's."

How could she explain so they'd understand why Elsie had kept the baby — so they'd know she wasn't a bad person?

"Elsie's baby, Alice, died last year, and that made her really sad. Fred says Elsie's mind plays tricks on her because of that. Elsie thought your baby was Alice, even though Alice is dead."

It sounded incredible, even to Lizzie. She looked at Elijah's mother, willing her to understand, but the woman only cradled Rose and frowned.

Bill's angry interruption startled Lizzie. "This is a load of codswallop! I want to talk about the lad."

"You'll get your turn soon enough," Elijah's grandfather said. "Let the lass speak."

"Colonel Clegg said you left the baby on purpose. He said you didn't deserve to have her. He said Elsie could keep her."

A man leaped to his feet. "Gorgios think they can do whatever they want. What gives them the right?"

Elijah's grandfather responded, "That's enough, Jeremiah. Don't frighten the girl."

The man sat down as quickly as he'd jumped up.

"Lizzie went against them others. She helped me get Rose back. She was brave," Elijah said.

Warmth tingled in Lizzie's toes and spread up her body until her face flushed with it. No one had ever called her *brave* before.

"Do you know owt about what happened with Bill?" Elijah's grandfather asked.

"Elijah told me Bill made him leave Rose in the field. He said Bill wanted Elijah to go and catch rabbits with him."

"She just wants to get Elijah out of trouble, Ambrose. She'll say whatever the lad told her." Bill's expression hardened. "I never said owt before because I didn't want to upset Vi, but her boy's no good. He's a Gorgio-lover. Thinks he's too good fer the likes of us. He's a wrong un."

Elijah's cheeks blazed red. "You're the wrong un. You blackmailed me and lied about it."

"You're the liar!" Bill thundered.

Elijah's mother's determined voice cut through the anger. "I asked you before and you didn't answer, so I'll ask you again, Bill." She stood and faced him with Rose in her arms. "Did you make Elijah leave Rose in that field?"

All the bluster left Bill. Guilt was written in his sideways glance; he didn't need to answer.

Elijah's mother spat at his feet. "You're a disgrace. I'm a married woman. Not fer all the coal in Yorkshire would I ever take up with you!"

A circle of solemn faces looked toward Elijah's grandfather. He focused on Bill. "There's been many a cold night when we've supped on rabbit you caught and listened to yer fiddle, Bill. But you've a mean streak and trouble follows you. Elijah's dad's off at the war, and you took advantage of that. You should be ashamed. When you blackmailed our Elijah and harmed the babby, you went too far." He pulled back his shoulders. "You wronged our Vi, and you wronged Elijah. Since his dad's not here, Elijah will choose yer fate."

Elijah stared Bill down. "I say we shun him." His voice was strong and firm as he pointed toward the gate. "Bill, leave us and don't never come back. You're dead to us."

"You can't shun me. The others'll not agree," Bill said.

Granddad Ambrose circled his arm around Elijah's shoulder. "When we get to the fair, we'll tell the others what you did. If I was you, Bill, I'd get far away from here as quick as you can."

"I'll settle up with you and yours one day, Ambrose," Bill said. "You'd best keep an eye out fer

me. And so should she; I've a debt to pay her, too."
He stabbed a finger at Lizzie.

The silent group watched as Bill led his horse
through the rutted mud by the gate. He climbed up
onto his wagon, turned, and raised his hand in an ob-
scene two-fingered gesture. Then he shook the reins
and moved off in the opposite direction to the village. The metallic sound of hoofbeats faded as he
crested the hill and disappeared from view.

Chapter Twenty-Seven

LIZZIE

THE GROUP of solemn Gypsies dispersed quietly. Lizzie was unsure what to do next. If she went back to Elsie's, she'd have to face Madge.

Elijah's mother climbed the yellow steps up to her wagon and opened the door. "Come on in, love. You look like you could do with a cuppa."

Lizzie followed her, removing her shoes and setting them side by side on the narrow porch before stepping over the threshold.

The cozy wagon wasn't any bigger than their bomb shelter at home, but whereas the shelter was filled with stark furnishings — such as camp beds and a portable stove — the wagon was homey and cheerful with bright cushions and rugs.

Lizzie squeezed between a little cabinet filled with pretty gold-rimmed china and a small black stove with a chimney pipe that poked up through the arched ceiling.

"Sit yerself down while I get the kettle on," Elijah's mother said, pointing to a chest beside a narrow oblong table.

Lizzie sat on a cushion on the chest and peeked through the lace-curtained window. She half expected to see Fred marching back to get her or, worse, Bill. But she only saw Elijah's grandfather tying a bicycle to the side of his wagon and a woman packing up cooking pots.

Elijah perched opposite Lizzie on a three-legged stool while his mother laid Rose on a raised bed at the other end of the wagon and tucked a blanket around her. There was only one bed. Did they all sleep in it? And where did they bathe? Or eat their meals? Or go to the toilet?

It would be rude to ask, so Lizzie stayed silent.

The kettle's shrill whistle pierced the quiet. Rose

threw her little arms in the air, but then sighed and went back to sleep. A curl of steam drifted from a sturdy brown teapot as Elijah's mother filled it with hot water.

"I'm sorry I took your baby," Lizzie blurted. "I didn't know it would cause all this trouble."

Elijah's mother paused in her task of pouring the tea. "Don't be sorry, pet. You did the right thing. You protected our Rose. It was them grownups were wrong. I don't see as how anyone could steal a babby. Some Gorgios think they can do anything."

Elijah smiled at Lizzie. "Lizzie's a Gorgio and she's not bad."

"Aye, she's different from most of them."

"Why is it so bad for a Gypsy and a . . . Gorgio . . . like me to be friends?" Lizzie asked.

"Most settled folk hates us. Even their bairns throw stones at us," Elijah's mother said. "It's best we stay separate. We have our customs. You have yours. The two don't mix."

Lizzie thought of the nasty things Mrs. Sidebottom, Madge, and the colonel had said about the Gypsies. It must be horrible if everywhere you went people called you names.

Elijah's mother gently interrupted Lizzie's thoughts. "Them folks that came here, are they yer family?"

Lizzie spoke quietly. "No. We're evacuees. We have to stay with them until the war's over."

"Where's yer own mam and dad, then?"

"Daddy's in the army, and Mummy's at home in Hull. We had to leave because of the bombs, but Mummy wasn't allowed to come with us."

"Well, yer mam an' dad can be proud of you," Elijah's mother said.

Lizzie sipped her tea. Its comforting warmth seeped into her. For the first time since arriving in Swainedale, she felt as if she was in a real home; but even though she wanted to, she couldn't stay — Peter would wonder what had happened to her. She didn't think Fred, Madge, or even Elsie would care.

"I'd better go now," she said, putting down her empty mug.

"Come and say goodbye to Rose before you goes," Elijah said

Rose sucked on her thumb as she slept. Her eyelids were as translucent as shells, and her dark hair curled over her delicate ears. Lizzie kissed her index finger and touched it to the baby's downy-soft cheek. Without her giggles and the silly nursery rhymes that Peter sang to her, Elsie's house would seem gloomier than ever.

Elijah's mother held out a carved wooden flower. "Take this. Ambrose makes them. It's not much, but it's summat to remember us by."

The flower's white petals surrounded a bright yellow center, just like the daisies in Mummy's garden. "Thank you. It's lovely," Lizzie said, holding the flower in front of her as if it were a whole bouquet.

She followed Elijah down the wagon steps and asked, "What will you do now?"

"We'll go to the fair. If we travel fast, we'll be there fer the last day. I want to see who bought my horse, my Lady."

Elijah tilted his head to one side and studied Lizzie. "You could come with us if you want. We can always make room fer another. You don't have to live with them folks."

Go with the Gypsies? Live in a home on wheels? Be a part of his family?

Lizzie tried to imagine that life. "If I come with

you, my parents won't know where I am." And what about Peter? She couldn't leave him on his own.

Elijah nodded, as if he'd known that would be her answer.

"Will you come back here after the fair?" she asked.

Elijah's dark curls bounced over his eyes when he shook his head. "Not blooming likely. That policeman'll have it in fer us, and Mammy'll never trust this place again. But I'll not forget you, Lizzie. You've been a good friend."

He fished something out of his pocket. "Take this fer luck."

Lizzie curled her fingers around the cool curve of Rose's horseshoe. She couldn't speak. She stood on tiptoe, kissed his cheek, then turned and ran down the lane.

Chapter Twenty-Eight

LIZZIE

LIZZIE TUCKED the horseshoe into her pocket. Her stomach heaved at the thought of facing Madge, and she slowed to a walk as she began the trek back up the dale. When she reached the row of houses, her meager supply of courage deserted her, and she hovered by Elsie's back door, holding her wooden flower.

The window curtain twitched and then the door opened.

Madge stood on the mat blocking the way. She screwed her eyebrows together and pursed her mouth. "It's about time you turned up." Then she stepped aside to let Lizzie in.

The small kitchen seemed to be full of people

and all of them angry at Lizzie. She took one step forward and stopped.

Peter broke the thick silence. "Elsie wants Alice back."

How could he still not understand?

Lizzie snapped at him. "The baby's Rose, not Alice. She's with her real family now."

But she regretted her sharp response when he hung his head and scuffed his foot against the tiles. His big toe poked out of a hole in his sock; Mummy would have mended a hole like that.

Words burst from Madge in an angry staccato. "After everything we did for you, this is how you pay us back."

Spittle collected at the corner of her mouth. "Never in my life ... deceitful ... you should be ashamed ... wicked ..." More words buzzed like wasps trapped in a jam jar.

"*You* made us tell lies. You're the wicked one. You're the one who should be ashamed." Once she'd begun, Lizzie couldn't stop. "Grownups are supposed to know what's right and wrong. You tried to steal Rose from her family, and you made us lie about it. That's wrong!"

Lizzie's chest heaved. For a moment, she struggled to breathe. She gripped the edge of the table for support. "I hate it here. I hate you. When I tell Mummy and Daddy what you've done, they'll report you. You should be put in jail."

Peter whimpered and moved closer to Elsie. She was a statue — as still as the stone cross on the moors. Her eyes were blank holes in her pale face.

Madge's face was purple with fury now. "How dare you speak to me like that? We took you in because there's a war on and we all have to do our bit. I should have known no good would come of it. You're an ungrateful little madam."

"And you're a mean old bat!"

Lizzie sucked in her breath. Surely she'd gone too far now.

"Now, then, let's all calm down," Fred said. "We don't want to do something we'll be sorry for later, do we?"

His mouth flattened into a line, and his face turned somber. "The Good Lord knows I'm no friend of the Gypsies, but I reckon that baby's rightfully theirs. I should've said that a long time ago. Could've saved us a lot of trouble."

Madge's voice shook. "I don't want our Elsie back the way she was." She dabbed at her eyes with a lace-fringed handkerchief. "The colonel can find these two somewhere else to stay. He can shove them in an orphanage for all I care. Good riddance to bad rubbish."

The words were harsh and bitter, but the tears — the tears were unexpected. Was Madge crying out of anger? Or sadness? Or fear for Elsie?

Fred circled his arm around Madge's shoulders. "Lizzie's just a child, love. Leave her be. She's had a lot to cope with, being sent away from home and all. She did the right thing, even if that pig did make a mess of my garden."

Elsie suddenly focused her gaze on Madge. Veins stood out like ropes on the backs of her thin hands as she reached out and stroked Peter's spiky hair. Her voice was a whisper. "I want them to stay, Madge. There's life in this house while they're here. I can't stand the quiet again."

Madge pressed her lips together.

"Lizzie was right about the baby. We shouldn't punish her for that." Elsie's voice was stronger now.

Madge stared hard at her sister. When she spoke, her words were brusque. "This is your house. You can do what you want. Don't come running to me when they get in trouble again."

But the faintest curve of a smile played over her lips. Even more surprising than the smile was the slight reassuring pat that Madge gave Lizzie's shoulder as she crossed Elsie's kitchen.

Baffled, Lizzie watched Madge march past the kitchen window toward her own back door.

Fred winked. "She's not a bad old stick. She'll come 'round. You'll see."

The door banged shut behind him.

Elsie unfolded her lean body and pushed herself up from her chair. She wrapped her arms around Lizzie and squeezed. "Don't mind about our Madge. She was only looking out for me."

Lizzie leaned into the hug and put her arms around Elsie's thin waist.

"You're a good girl, Lizzie," Elsie said. Then she filled a pan with water and set it on the stove. "Who's hungry? I've a mind for a boiled egg."

When her egg was ready, Lizzie picked off tiny shards of shell and ate the glistening dome of white before dipping a strip of bread into the runny yolk. The taste of the first eggy bite was so familiar, it overwhelmed her with memories of her father reading the newspaper at breakfast and her mother frying bacon. She gulped and swallowed.

"We're going to have to see about school for you two," Elsie said. "The village school's not big enough for all the evacuees. I'll have to ask Fred what arrangements have been made."

"Do we have to go to school?" Peter asked.

Nodding, Elsie ruffled his hair.

While Lizzie chewed her last bite of bread, the letterbox rattled.

Elsie held out the letter she retrieved from the doormat. "It's for you two."

Lizzie tore at the crackling envelope and pulled out a single sheet of paper.

Dear Lizzie and Peter,

I got your letter and I know you're homesick. I'll come and see you as soon as I can get a train ticket, and I'll bring Nana with me. We'll have a picnic and look at all those sheep you told us about.

Lots of love, Mummy

"I'll take her to see Curly!" Peter said. "And the cows. And the sheep."

Lizzie thought about what she'd tell her mother — about Elijah and how she'd helped him rescue his sister. She'd done the right thing. She was sure of it now. Her mother would be proud. And Nana, too. *That's my girl, Lizzie. You showed them.* That's what Nana would say.

Elsie interrupted Lizzie's reverie. "Who wants to come to the shop with me? I'm almost out of tea."

Peter bounced up and down on his toes. "I'll come. And can we go fishing, 'cos I haven't done that yet."

Lizzie grinned. "We can fish from the bridge. Let's bring Sam, too."

GLOSSARY

BAIRN: A child.

BECK: A stream.

BLACKOUT CURTAIN: A thick black window covering used during World War II to prevent any light inside a house from being seen outside.

BOMB SHELTER: A protected place to shelter people during air raids. Anderson shelters, like the one in Lizzie's back garden, were made out of corrugated metal panels and were partially buried in the ground and covered with soil.

BRACKEN: A large fern, or group of ferns.

COB: A big, strong, usually gentle horse bred to pull Gypsy wagons. Gypsy cobs are often white with black or brown spots. They have long "feathers" of hair flowing from their knees over their hooves.

CRICKET: A game played with a flat-sided wooden bat and a

hard ball. The batter scores runs by running between pieces of wood called wickets.

DALE: A valley.

DOUBLE-DECKER BUS: A bus with an upper and lower floor. The upper floor is reached using a staircase.

DRY STONE WALL: A wall made from stones of different sizes and shapes. No mortar is used to hold the stones together.

EVACUATE: To send people from one place to another to avoid danger.

EVACUEE: Someone who is evacuated.

GROUSE BLIND: Cover where hunters hide from the grouse they are hunting.

HEATHER: A bushy plant with small leaves and tiny pink or purple bell-shaped flowers.

HOB: A male ferret.

HORSE BRASS: An ornament made out of brass used to decorate a horse. Horse brasses may be hung from a horse's harness, over its forehead, or on its chest.

JILL: A female ferret.

KUSHTI: A Gypsy/Traveler word meaning "good."

MOOR: A large area of open, hilly land that can't be farmed. Often boggy, moorland has few trees and is covered in grass and heather.

NAPPY: A diaper.

PETROL: Gasoline.

POACHER: A person who trespasses on someone else's land and steals game such as pheasants and grouse.

PRAM: A four-wheeled baby carriage with a hood.

PRIVY: An outdoor toilet.

RATIONING: An allowance of something such as food. In World War II England, petrol, clothing, and food such as butter, sugar, and meat were rationed by the government.

SATCHEL: A school bag (usually made of leather) with a buckle and shoulder strap.

SHUN: To reject or send a person away as a punishment.

STILE: A step or series of steps to help someone climb over a wall.

TRAVELER: A person who moves from place to place and does not have a permanent home. Other names for Travelers are Gypsies, Rom, Roma, or Romani.

ACKNOWLEDGMENTS

Lizzie and the Lost Baby is a work of fiction grounded in the reality of events that took place in England during World War II, when three and a half million people, most of them children, were evacuated from British cities and towns considered to be at risk from German bombing raids. The evacuated children were sent to live with strangers, often for the duration of the war. My father and uncle were two of those evacuees. Swainedale, the valley in my story, can't be found on any map, but it most closely resembles Rosedale in the North York Moors, where my parents have owned a cottage for many years.

Writing a book is a thrilling, arduous, exasperating, and lonely task, but I received abundant encouragement and assistance and owe thanks to many people. The greatest debt is to my parents, Ernie and Joan Connolly, first for nurturing my love of the Yorkshire countryside and second for sharing their wartime memories with me. Until I began writing this story I had not realized that my father was evacuated to the countryside and lived away from his parents for four years and that my mother stayed in Hull with my widowed grandmother and endured frequent bombing raids in a cramped bomb shelter.

I am deeply indebted to Ann Rider, my editor, for her gentle insistence on subtlety and for helping me focus the story on what matters most — Lizzie's emotional journey. I also owe a huge debt of gratitude to my friend, mentor, and teacher, Jane Resh Thomas. Her emphasis on connecting the plot line to the emotion line helped me make this a better story. I "do my work," but Jane inspires me to learn, experiment, and try harder.

Thanks go to my agent, Tina Wexler, for loving this book and supporting me as I strove to make it the best it could be, and also to the generous Twin Cities literary community, especially Pat Schmatz and Kurtis Scaletta, whose enthusiastic support spurred me on. I am grateful for the unending encouragement and assistance of my fellow workshop and critique group members who read chapters, offered perceptive feedback, and cheered me on every step of the way.

Ideas and inspiration came from Maggie Smith-Bendell's memoir, *Rabbit Stew and a Penny or Two: A Gypsy Family's Hard Times and Happy Times on the Road in the 1950s*. I can't thank Maggie enough for reading an early draft of my story and encouraging me to continue.

Becca Stadtlander's sweet cover finally brought home the reality that this story would become an actual book! I am grateful to her for her delicious illustration.

Last, but never least, special thanks go to my family: to David, who never complains about my whining and offers only support and encouragement; and to Eleanor and Ben, who when we uprooted them from their home in Yorkshire and moved them to America, accepted the challenge of their new lives — much as the evacuees did.